D1542252

THE CASE OF THE WEEPING WITCH

BY THE SAME AUTHOR

(MCGURK MYSTERIES)

The Nose Knows

Deadline for McGurk

The Case of the Condemned Cat

The Case of the Nervous Newsboy

The Great Rabbit Rip-Off

The Case of the Invisible Dog

The Case of the Secret Scribbler

The Case of the Phantom Frog

The Case of the Treetop Treasure

The Case of the Snowbound Spy

The Case of the Bashful Bank Robber

The Case of the Four Flying Fingers

McGurk Gets Good and Mad

The Case of the Felon's Fiddle

The Case of the Slingshot Sniper

The Case of the Vanishing Ventriloquist

The Case of the Muttering Mummy

The Case of the Wandering Weathervanes

The Case of the Purloined Parrot

(MCGURK FANTASIES)

The Case of the Dragon in Distress

The Case of the Weeping Witch

A McGurk Fantasy

BY E. W. HILDICK

Macmillan Publishing Company   New York

Maxwell Macmillan Canada   Toronto

Maxwell Macmillan International
New York   Oxford   Singapore   Sydney

Macmillan Publishing Company is part of the Maxwell Communication
Group of Companies.

Macmillan Publishing Company
866 Third Avenue, New York, NY 10022

Maxwell Macmillan Canada, Inc.
1200 Eglinton Avenue East, Suite 200
Don Mills, Ontario M3C 3N1

First edition
Printed in the United States of America

10 9 8 7 6 5 4 3 2 1

The text of this book is set in 12 point Caledonia.

Library of Congress Cataloging-in-Publication Data
Hildick, E. W. (Edmund Wallace), date.
     The case of the weeping witch : a McGurk fantasy / by E.W.
Hildick—1st ed.
          p.   m.
     Summary: While working on a school project, the members of the
McGurk Organization travel back to 1692 and find themselves
involved in charges of witchcraft.
     ISBN 0-02-743785-X
     [1. Time travel—Fiction.   2. Witchcraft—Fiction.]   I. Title.
     PZ7.H5463Cavp   1992   [Fic]—dc20   91-38231

To
Carol Hoffman and Jane Kates
of The House of Books, Kent, Connecticut
and
Edwina Amarosa
of the Kent Center School Library
whose help with the background research
for this book
has been invaluable
and greatly appreciated.

Contents

1   Many Questions—and One Answer   13

2   Hester Bidgood—Investigatrix   20

3   The Voice   27

4   Hester's Casebook   35

5   Blazing Scalp Again   41

6   One Half of a Dragon   47

7   The Six New Pilgrims   53

8   Jacob Peabody   59

9   The Knife of Many Uses   70

10   Client in Distress   77

11   Hester's Flight   85

12   Rob MacGregor   92

13   Jacob Peabody's "Evill Deedes"   97

14   Rob's Report   106

15   Blazing Scalp's Lodge   112

16   The Rescue   123

17   Peacemaker Makes a Deal   130

18   The Witchfinder Found   141

19   New Light on Hester   151

THE CASE OF THE WEEPING WITCH

1 Many Questions— and One Answer

This was a case which bristled with mysteries. Deep, dark questions like:

Was young Hester Bidgood *really* a witch?

Did they hang her for it?

Why was the powerful landowner and magistrate, Jacob Peabody, so keen to have her arrested?

Who was Jacob Peabody's mysterious guest—the one he got to help him in his evil plans?

Why did Jacob Peabody keep his guest so closely under wraps, hiding him in a root cellar and a dark, windowless attic room?

Plus:

How come Mistress Brown—the oldest inhabitant of our town in 1692—knew who we were, the moment she saw us?

For that matter, how come we turned up there that night, three hundred years ago?

And indeed:

Would we all get back? Would one of us, or some of us, get arrested and hung for being witches ourselves?

Funnily enough, it all started with the answer to an everyday twentieth-century mystery. One that had been bugging us for years:

What did our leader's middle initial stand for? Jack *P.* McGurk?

He was always flashing it around. Especially when he signed his name in that fancy, curly handwriting:

Jack P. McGurk

But it was no use asking him. He'd usually pretend he hadn't heard, with his green eyes blinking out of his mask of freckles. Either that or he'd say, "That's *my* business." Or, "That's a question that only gets answered on a need-to-know basis."

Some of us didn't give up easily. We used to throw out guesses, suggesting that the *P* stood for Peter or Patrick, or even Phillip or Phineas. Then we'd look hard at his face, hoping he'd give away his secret by a flicker of the eyes.

But no. It seemed he was as good at concealing clues as spotting them.

In fact, it was Ms. Ellis, our teacher, who cracked it. Right at the beginning of her project: *Life in Our Area Three Hundred Years Ago.*

"Many of those early Puritans didn't like frills in anything," she said. "Not even in their children's names."

Then she reeled off a few examples. Girls who got lumbered with handles like Charity or Mercy or Gracious or Humble. And guys with Reformation or Discipline or Praise-God.

That's when I noticed McGurk beginning to squirm. And the squirming got even squirmier when Ms. Ellis went on:

"Some of those names weren't *too* outlandish. Some are still in use today, like Prudence or Hope. I was interested to discover only yesterday, going through your records, that *you* have one, Jack McGurk, and I must say that the fine old name Perseverance suits you very—"

She didn't get any further, what with McGurk leaping to his feet, his face almost as red as his hair, protesting, "But Ms. Ellis—!" and horselaughs from jerks like Sandra Ennis, and even some kinder laughs from—well, I have to admit—some of his fellow officers of the McGurk Organization.

"Oh, dear!" said Ms. Ellis, frowning us into something

like silence. "I had no idea it was a secret, Jack. But, you know, Perseverance *does* suit you very well, judging from what I hear of your skill as a detective."

Well, naturally, that pacified him some. Still red around the ears, he even managed a smirk. And, quick to follow up—not to mention *cover* up—Ms. Ellis went immediately into the subject of witches and witch-hunts. This put the subject of weird names right to the back of our minds. Even McGurk's.

I mean, the craziness and cruelty of it all was bad enough. The tortures and the tests they put those poor people to. But it was the sheer injustice that got to McGurk most.

It was still eating him that afternoon, when the McGurk Organization met in his basement, our HQ. . . .

But first he had to clear up the name business—sort of take the sting out of being called Perseverance. How? By involving *us* in it, that's how.

"I like the idea, men," he said, as we sat at the old round table. "Having names that match your skills."

So there and then he started dishing them out.

"You, Officer Joey Rockaway," he said to me, "would be called Recorder. Short for Recorder-of-the-Truth."

Well, fair enough. After all, that's my main job. Recording all the facts of our cases.

Willie Sandowsky wasn't so sure, however, when McGurk dubbed him Sniffer.

"Sniffer?" he said, fingering his long nose.

"Short for Sniffer-Out-of-the-Truth," said McGurk.

Willie relaxed. His very sensitive sense of smell *has* helped crack many a case.

So McGurk went on, renaming Brains Bellingham, our science expert, Measurer (short for Measurer-of-the-Truth); and Wanda Grieg, Climber (Climber-to-the-Truth), because she's the Organization's best scaler of trees, walls, or even buildings in the course of duty. Finally, Mari Yoshimura drew the name Speaker (short for Speaker-of-the-Truth-in-Many-Tongues), on account of her ability to throw her voice and imitate other people's voices.

By then, McGurk was ready to deal with the sheer injustice of witch-hunting.

"Just think of it, men," he said. "Branding some orone as a felon simply because they have a birthmark or something similar! With the death penalty in force!"

We all growled in agreement.

"I mean," said McGurk, "I bet if *we'd* been around then, we could all have been accused of witchcraft on *those* crummy grounds. Right?"

And before we knew it, he had us confessing to birthmarks, some of which we'd managed to keep quiet about until then.

He was so serious he even had me charting them, typing it out, with drawings. Here's a copy:

SO-CALLED WITCHMARKS BELONGING TO PERSONNEL OF THE McGURK
ORGANIZATION

Chief McGurk

+ Red hair (always suspect
  in those days.)
+ Bunch of freckles, back
  of right hand, joining to
  form butterfly shape.

Officer Rockaway

+ Mole, kite-shaped. (Chief M.
  says more like scales of
  justice, but it depends which
  way up you look at it.)
  $3\frac{1}{2}$" above left knee.

Officer Yoshimura

+ She says none, but Chief M.
  says her hair is the
  blackest he has ever seen,
  and keen witch-hunters
  could use it against her.

Officer Grieg

+ Mole, just below left
  shoulder, shaped like a
  clover leaf.

Officer Sandowsky

+ He says none, but Chief M.
  says his nose would be
  enough to mark him for a
  witch any day.

Officer Bellingham

+ Purple mole, shaped like a
  sitting mouse, high on
  right thigh.

There were some objections. Brains was reluctant to show us his, even after Willie had said he'd seen it lots of times at the pool. And Wanda refused to call hers either a witchmark *or* a mole.

"It's a *beauty* spot!" she said, with a backward toss of her long yellow hair.

"It isn't what *you* call it, Officer Grieg," said McGurk. "It's what a witch-hunter would call it. . . . And you'd have had to stop doing *that,* too."

"Doing what?"

"Tossing your hair back. You heard what Ms. Ellis said. Even *that* was taken for a witch sign."

That silenced Wanda. In fact, it silenced us all. It was almost as if McGurk had already decided that this was to be the destination of our second Time Mission. Southern New England in 1692. Like he was already putting us on our guard about those birthmarks and other features that could so easily land us in jail.

Or even on the gallows . . .

2 Hester Bidgood— Investigatrix

Those weren't the only preparations, either.

Over the next few days, McGurk's interest became keener. Ms. Ellis encouraged us to do our own research in both the school and the town libraries. There wasn't much material about our town itself, but there was quite a lot about life in seventeenth century New England. So, gradually, we built up a picture of things like the farming methods and houses and furniture and stuff. Not forgetting the way people dressed and spoke and their dealings with the Indians.

Naturally, most of the kids tended to concentrate on Indian raids and the wolves and bears that roamed around. And, of course, witches. So Ms. Ellis had to steer them into studying the more ordinary everyday things as well.

She had a surprise helper in this.

"She's right, men," McGurk said. "I want you to find out all you can about the background. Like you, Officer Rockaway—you should be studying the words they used."

"I already am," I said.

"And you, Officer Yoshimura, the way they spoke."

"I am trying, Chief McGurk, but it is not easy without tape recordings."

"As for you, Officer Grieg . . ."

And so he went on, urging us to study things like farms and crops and forests, in Wanda's case; and tools and instruments and weapons, in Brains's; and food in Willie's (the senses of taste and smell being very close).

I could guess at McGurk's purpose. The guy *was* getting us briefed for a possible time trip. Ms. Ellis's aims were much simpler. She wanted us to prepare ten-minute presentations to round off the project—talks on our chosen subjects.

Well, there were some really wild ones, but McGurk's was the wildest and wackiest. I mean *he'd* concentrated on witch-hunting, and one witch-hunter in particular. The only snag was that this guy had operated a long, long way from New England.

"His name was Matthew Hopkins," he told the class. "He made a fat living out of it. And if *I'd* had anything to do with it, this is the sort of notice I'd have put up in every post office—"

"They didn't have post offices in those days!" Sandra Ennis chimed in.

"In stores and taverns, then," said McGurk, as he unrolled the poster he'd been working on at home.

There was a gasping and a murmuring as we crowded around to get a better look at McGurk's handiwork.

Here's a copy:

WANTED

Matthew Hopkins
calls himself
Witch Finder Generall
a.k.a.
RACKETEER SUPREME

M.O. Goes around ~(falsely)~ accusing people of being witches. Gets money
(a) for just visiting a town or village
(b) plus extra for each person he claims to be a witch and has put to death.

This = **MURDER FOR MONEY**
(= MURDER INCORPORATED)

Other Scams   (~possibly~ probably)
BLACKMAIL — threatening to accuse people if they don't pay him to keep quiet.

While I was gaping at this, McGurk was filling the audience in.

"This man was responsible for hundreds of people being executed," he said. "And the victims didn't stand a chance. One of his tests was to tie the suspects up, wrap them in a sheet or a blanket, and chuck them in the river. If they floated, he said that proved they were guilty. If they sank, they were innocent. Innocent but also dead, of course! Drowned! But he got his, in the end. Someone accused *him* of being a witch, and they found a witchmark on him. So they gave him his own water test. Which he failed."

"Yes, but—" Sandra Ennis began.

"There were also so-called witchfinders in Scotland—"

"Yes," Sandra broke in again. "But these lived in Scotland or England. Not over here in *New* England."

"I *know!*" said McGurk. "But it was around the same time. And I bet there were racketeers just like them here. With a scam like that, there just had to be some rats who'd take advantage of it. It's only that no one ever found them out, is all."

Sandra sneered.

"Which *you* would have done, of course! You and your crummy Organization. If you'd been around."

"You're darned right we would!" said McGurk.

"Fat chance!" jeered Sandra. "And anyway, there were no witches hunted in *this* town!"

"Oh, no?"

"No!"

"How do *you* know?"

"There aren't any records of any," she said.

McGurk turned.

"Is that right, Officer Rockaway?"

"Well," I said, "lots of records can have been destroyed in three hundred years. Just because there aren't any—"

"What do *you* know about it?" sneered Sandra. "You say anything the jerk wants you to, *Officer* Rockaway!"

"That's enough!" said Ms. Ellis.

I guess she thought it was getting out of hand.

In fact, maybe that's why she did some research herself and came up with some new information the next day. Something that brought McGurk's attention right back from Old England.

"It seems we did have a case of witchcraft here after all, class," she said, glancing at some notes. "I went over to the town hall yesterday afternoon and, sure enough, the records for that period have nearly all been destroyed or lost. But there was one scrap—it was charred at the edges—dated October 21, 1692."

She began to write on the board.

" '*Arrested this day, Hester Bidgood, aged 13, charged with witchcraft after claiming to be*'—and this is how it was spelled—'*an Investigatrix of Evill Deedes, and also after being descried performing sundry acts during the hours of darkness, viz.*—' " Ms. Ellis sighed. "And there, I'm afraid, the entry ends."

"It sounds she was more like a witch-hunter herself, miss," I said. "If 'investigatrix' means some kind of investigator."

"It does," said Ms. Ellis. "A female investigator."

Well, that puzzzled us all. But straight after school, we went to the public library reference room and looked the word up in the big twelve-volume English dictionary. "There," I said, " 'Investigatrix. A word no longer used, but in the seventeenth century it meant' "—I peered closer, because this part was in very small print—" 'She which tracketh.' "

"Ugh!" said Wanda. "Sounds creepy!"

"And here," I said. "Another reference: 'Investigatours, or *crafty searchers*.' "

"*That* sounds witchy!" said Willie.

"Witchy my foot!" said McGurk. His eyes were gleaming. "That's what *they* might have thought. But all it means is that Hester was really a private detective. Eh, Officer Rockaway? I mean, maybe they didn't have the word 'detective' yet, huh?"

"They didn't," I said.

"So what are you looking so gloomy about?" he said.

"I'm just thinking how, witchmarks or no witchmarks, *we'd* have been accused of witchcraft, too," I said. "Just for making the very same claim as she did."

Wanda looked very uneasy.

"I—I wonder what happened to her?" she said.

"Hung, probably," said Willie.

Brains pushed his glasses back along his nose.

"Well, we don't know that for sure," he said.

"There's one way we *could* find out, men," said McGurk. "If only the walkie-talkies would do what they did before."

We looked at each other—some doubtful, some hopeful, some plain scared.

Then Mari spoke up.

"Let us at least try, Chief McGurk. Please! Maybe we will be able to help this poor girl. It—well—it is our *duty*."

That settled it.

"You bet it is, Officer Yoshimura!" said McGurk. "We make our move tonight!"

3 The Voice

The walkie-talkies were a bunch of six that our science expert's uncle had given him. They'd been bought in a junk store's fire sale, and at first, not even Brains could get them to work. So he opened them up and made some changes, and that hadn't seemed to work, either. Not during the daytime, anyway. But when he tried them after dark, he did manage to get a buzzing sound.

That's when McGurk decided to use them for the Organization. So that we could talk to each other at night, in bed. Result: zilch again. Only the humming noise.

At first.

But in the small hours, after we'd nodded off, *then* they worked. Boy, did they ever! Because that's when we found ourselves transported back eight centuries and four thousand miles. Near to a medieval castle on the border of England and Wales. I recorded it all in "The Case of the Dragon in Distress," and one very hairy adventure that was. We were lucky to get back from it alive, if you ask me.

That was several weeks ago. At first, none of us were keen on trying it out again. Then some of the others began to show a renewed interest. Willie, for instance, hankered after a trip to Ancient Egypt. Wanda and Mari had a mind to go back to the French Revolution—to Paris, France. No luck in either case.

Then Brains got the idea that the walkie-talkies would only work as time machines when we wished to go someplace where we understood the language. So he opted for Philadelphia at the time when Benjamin Franklin was making his inventions. And that was another no-no. Maybe Brains's choice was a bit tame, we thought. But the result was just the same when we tried with McGurk's: Chicago in the 1920s, in the days of the gangster Al Capone.

So why should it happen *this* time?

Well, maybe it was because of knowing the background so thoroughly. Or maybe it was the place itself— with only the time to have to travel through and no regular distance at all.

Or maybe it was because we'd all been so concerned about the plight of that innocent kid.

It worked, anyway.

Mind you, at first it didn't seem like it would. My walkie-talkie made the same faint but unbroken hissing noise for hours. Just once, before I fell asleep, it did give a little spurt, and I fancied I heard a far-off voice saying,

"And you shall be put to the test!" But that was all, until suddenly I woke up with a start, in pitch-blackness, shivering with cold.

And then, when I put out an arm to grab the bed covers and felt only something thin and bony, and a voice, Willie's, said, "Hey! That's my nose!" and I opened my eyes and sat up—only then did I realize what had happened.

I saw a crescent moon, stars, black branches of trees, dim crouching shapes and heard another voice: "Keep *quiet*, Officer Sandowsky!"

"McGurk?" I whispered, getting to my feet.

"Yeah," one of the shapes replied. "And now we're all present, maybe we'll be mission capable. . . . Is your set switched on?"

I felt at my side, to where the walkie-talkie was hanging. The switch was on the *receive* position. Fumbling around, I was glad to note that I'd made the journey fully dressed, in my street clothes. It was pretty chilly under those trees.

"Yes," I said. "Where are we?"

The sets crackled. Mine and five others. And out of them came a voice, not loud but very clear, saying "You are standing at what *you* know as the intersection of River Road and Park."

We stirred uneasily in the undergrowth, where there didn't seem to be even a path. That intersection is the busiest in town, day and night. A traffic black-spot, in fact, where you could easily get yourself killed.

Willie gulped. "You mean this—*this* is our home town?"

"Aye!" the Voice answered testily. "But the year is 1692."

It wasn't quite the same Voice as last time. It was thinner and brisker and more worried sounding. And very impatient.

"And might I add that 'tis high time you all got here, slow-bellies, *high* time! The little maid is due to be cried out as a witch *any* day now!"

"Sorry, sir—uh—sire!" said McGurk. "But—"

"Silence!" snapped the Voice. "I am about to tell you of your mission. . . ." The tone softened some. "The maid does not know it yet for sure. But she suspects that something goes sadly amiss. Her nerve strings are tight, very tight. Tight nigh unto snapping. See you tread gently with her."

"We—we understand, sir," Wanda murmured.

"Sure," said McGurk. "We—"

"Your mission," the Voice went on, "is to rescue her from an unjust accusation and a certain terrible death."

"Leave it to us, sire!" said McGurk, sounding more confident all at once.

" 'Twill not be easy," said the Voice. "And know this. You yourselves will also be in terrible peril of your lives."

He then went on to speak of what he called our "black boxes" and our "preternatural sense of smells" and our "art of the ventriloque" (by which I guessed he meant Mari's voice throwing).

"You will be in great danger if you try to use them to impress these people or to affright them, as you did on your last mission."

"Sire!" gasped McGurk. "But why? We'd never have made it without them!"

"No matter," said the Voice. "The people in England at *that* time thought they were magic, aye. But they were used to believing in magic. They even welcomed it as a diversion." His tone darkened. "But these people are different. To them all magic is 'the Work of the Devil.' You would be put to death as witches yourselves. Instantly."

"But," McGurk began, with a yelp of protest in his voice, "they—"

"Use the boxes by all means," said the Voice. "But privily, normally, to communicate one to the other."

Mari, who'd been studying costumes of the period, as well as accents, said, "What about our clothes? Will they not think we are witches because of the strange way we dress?"

"An excellent question, my dear," said the Voice. "And one that must be taken care of before all others. . . . Now there is in this settlement a woman—one Mistress

Brown—who will help you in such matters and who doth half expect you. And—Ah! Here comes Hester Bidgood now!"

We turned. Our eyes must have been getting more used to the darkness. I saw that we were actually near the edge of a clearing. In that clearing were some glimmers of light. Thin glimmers, mere lines of light from behind the shutters of a small house. With another smaller but rounder glimmer getting steadily bigger, three or four feet from the ground.

And now, as it drew nearer, we saw it was a lantern, held by someone roughly our own height, in a long, dark dress with a splash of white above—a bonnet or cap. She stopped in front of a denser patch of darkness, which turned out to be a hut.

As the newcomer opened a creaking door and stepped inside, I realized the boxes had gone silent. Only the breathing of the other guys made a sound. That and the soft splash and murmur of a river, somewhere in the near distance.

"A diagonal approach, men," whispered McGurk, leading the way.

So we crept stealthily up to the side of that hut. There was no window, but there were plenty of cracks, and we were able to get a good view of our latest client.

And yes. She was about thirteen years old, I guessed, though she looked a few years older. That was because she looked so grave and anxious, as she sat on a heap of logs and opened a book. In fact, she was rather homely, with a receding chin and bulging eyes. Only her hair was what you might call pretty—a bright, lively red as it peeped in curls from under the white, frilly cap. Rather like McGurk's hair, come to think of it, but curlier and, as I say, prettier.

Willie stifled a sneeze. He made a fairly good job of muting it, but it startled Hester. She *must* have been a bag of nerves, the way the book shot out of her hand and she jumped to her feet.

But she was spunky, I'll give her that.

Without any further hesitation, she picked up the lantern and went to the door.

"Remember what the Voice said, men," whispered McGurk. "Try not to scare her."

She was already at the open door, lantern lifted, peering out.

Then she said, in a soft but carrying voice, "Be that you, Blazing Scalp?"

My blood seemed to freeze. We hadn't even moved out of the deep shadows.

Was she addressing McGurk?

Could she see the color of his hair even in the dark? Was she *really* a witch?

Then McGurk stepped forward.

"The name's McGurk actually," he said, in his oiliest

tones. "Do not worry, ma'am—young ma'am—we hath come to help thou!'

In the lantern light I saw a slight frown, then a flicker of hope in those bulging eyes.

"Cut it out, McGurk," I said. "There's no need to talk gibberish. She can understand us if we talk straight."

The flicker brightened to a glow.

"Come—come in," she whispered.

Then all at once, the flicker got doused in a flood of tears, and she staggered across to the logs and sank down on them, her shoulders shaking with harsh, racking sobs.

It seemed like we'd made contact with the weeping "witch" all right!

4 Hester's Casebook

While the rest were bunching around trying to console her, with Wanda in the lead, I picked up Hester's book. It had a thick paperboard cover with a brown, white, and red whirly sort of pattern. And, being the word expert of the Organization, I was naturally interested to glance inside and see what sort of stuff kids used to read in those days.

Well, it wasn't that kind of book. It was for writing in. In fact, it was Hester's notebook, carefully written in black ink.

And McGurk had been right. These weren't notes about witch happenings. They looked much more like the ordinary case notes of a regular detective. Rather like the ones *I* make.

So I guess it wasn't all that wrong of me to do a little dipping while the others were busy with the sobbing client. I mean:

1. It was a purely professional interest, one expert seeing how it was done by another.

And 2. It was also *evidence*. It proved that just because she called herself something spooky like an "investigatrix," it didn't make her a witch.

I only glanced at a few pages, anyway. But I have to admit that I made notes of them later that night, while they were fresh in my memory. By then I'd realized they might be important. In fact, I've got Mari to copy them out, using the same sort of handwriting as Hester's—which Mari is good at.

Here for starters is the title page:

Hester Bidgood
Investigatrix
of
Evill Deedes
Her Book

(Reconstructed by
J.R + M. Y.)

Then there was the first page of the entries:

Cause No. 1

The Stealing and Stoning of
Goody Willson's her Kitten

The evill doer of this evill
deede was

Peacemaker
Cleary.

I discovered this when I
investigated on Friday,
the fifteenth day of

Peacemaker Cleary didn't mean anything to me just then, so I went on flipping through until I came to this:

Cause No. 5.

Evill deedes done by

Mr. Jacob Peabody

to my true
and certain
knowledge

Whick I am still
investigating.

And then this last entry, which began:

> Cause No. 7
>
> *The Mysteriouse Guest of Mr. Peabody.*
> He hath No Name that I know on, but I did catch a glympse of his face and he was no right man, he was horride.
> This was yestere'en when I was with

But here I got no further, because she jumped up and sprang across and snatched back the book.

"Give me that!" she almost snarled.

"Sorry, Hester!" I said. "It's just that we are detectives, too—uh—investigatours and investigatrixes—and—uh—"

She was back on her pile of logs sobbing again, clutching the book to her chest, with both hands crossed over it.

"Hey, take it easy, Hester!" McGurk was saying. "We've come here to save you! They're going to accuse you of being a *witch*!"

"Y-yes," she said, between sobs. "But—don't you see—I—I *must* be a witch if I can see and con-converse with creatures like you!"

"But we're *not* creatures!" said McGurk. "We're flesh and blood human beings! It's only that we've traveled back three hundred years in—"

"McGurk!" warned Wanda.

But it was too late. McGurk's words had caused Hester to set up the biggest howl yet. And when it subsided and she'd gotten some kind of a grip on herself, she groaned and said: "Even—even if that is true, look at you, dressed like that! If they see me merely *talking* to you I shall be arrested and tested!"

She had a point there, I guess. Even in the dim light our clothes did seem kind of bright and—well—way-out, compared to hers.

"But we're here to *help!*" McGurk persisted. "We—we're the McGurk Organization. I'm—uh—*Persever-ance* McGurk. And these are my officers."

His crafty use of his middle name seemed to help, being the sort of name she was used to. She blinked a few tears away at any rate and appeared to be listening closer.

"And about our clothes," McGurk went on, "the Voice told us—"

"McGurk!" Wanda warned again.

"Our—uh—adviser—uh—Watch Commander—he

told us before we came that a Mistress Smith would help us take care of the clothes problem."

"That's Mistress *Brown*," I said.

"Yeah, well, whatever—" McGurk went on. "It—"

But he had to stop. For the first time since we'd shown ourselves, Hester was smiling through her tears.

"Oh!" she said. "Oh, you should have told me before! Now *she* is my godmother. If *she* is prepared to help you, you *must* be genuine and true!"

She stood up, still clutching her book.

"But I fear 'tis getting late," she said. "Happily, she lives quite close. Come with me and I will show you the way."

As we followed her into the chilly night air, I thought I caught a glimpse of a dark figure, lurking nearby. But by the time I'd blinked and narrowed my eyes, it had gone, melted into the shadows. I put it down to imagination plus some steam on my glasses.

Just as long as it isn't Mr. Peabody's "mysterious guest!" I thought, with a slight shudder and a last backward glance. . . .

5 Blazing Scalp Again

Since those days, our town has grown to many times the original size. Now it sprawls on both sides of the river, with a busy downtown section, two industrial areas, and several neighborhoods. At the center is Willow Park, on steeply rising ground in a bend in the river, the only part that is almost the same now as it was then.

In those days, the town was just a huddle of houses built on land that had been cleared in the forest to the east of the river. Beyond the houses to the north and south were fields, with a few homesteads here and there, most of them tiny, but one or two closer to the town, quite big. The south fields were owned by ordinary townsfolk, land that had been split up and shared out. The north fields belonged to a few wealthier landowners, mostly people whose parents and grandparents had gotten here first.

But in 1692 that was all there was. The river was the frontier. The whole of the west side was dense forest. Wanda had made a good job of mapping out the township, with the help of some old books and records, and Ms.

Ellis had given her a straight A for it. Here is a copy of that sketch map, with a few additions made later, including Hester's hut and homestead and Mistress Brown's house. Also the points marked X and Y and Z, which were to play such a vital part in our mission.

N

FOREST

FIELDS

Hester's Aunt's House

Mistress Brown's

FIELDS

River path

FOREST (WILLOW PARK)

High Ground

FOREST

FOREST (with small clearings)

Jacob Peabody's

⊗ Main Street

Forest track to East

River path FIELDS

◇

FOREST

Creek FOREST

Swamp

Ⓩ

FOREST

W. G.

Ⓗ = Hester's Hut

⊗ⓎⓏ = Points of Life or Death Importance to Hester Bidgood

As we walked along a dirt road on the way to Mistress Brown's that first night, I managed to get a rough idea of my bearings, thanks to that map and what the Voice had told us. It was very spooky and dark. The only lights came from the little township and nothing at all from the dense bulk of the land ahead across the river—where the sky in our time is usually lit up with the glow from thousands of sources. The ground we were crossing wasn't a part of where we go much nowadays, but I had an idea there were some kind of senior citizens' homes there.

In fact, Hester quite startled me when she said, "This is her house. And please to remember she is very old and might have gone to bed, even though 'tis only a little after seven o' clock."

A chain rattled and a dog began to growl.

"Good boy!" said Hester, and the animal's growl turned into whimpers of greeting.

Hester led us to a lighted window.

"Good!" she murmured. "She has not retired yet, after all. That is she in the chair by the fire."

We crowded forward. The window glass was coarse and blurry. All I could see was what looked like a bundle of shawls. Then I made out a white-capped head that was tilted forward, as if its wearer were listening for something or had fallen asleep.

McGurk made a doubtful grunting noise. I could guess what he was thinking. If this was the lady we were depending on for support, we'd come about fifty years too late!

"See that you do not startle her too much," said Hester. "'Tis somewhat of a dragon she be when tired. . . . But she is very *kind*," she added.

"We *were* told she'd be half expecting us," Wanda murmured.

Hester glanced at Wanda, then at the rest of us. She shook her head. "I will leave you to your business with her," she said. "Go knock on the door—not too loud— and her servant Nell will announce you, if . . ." She sighed. "I wish you success. I do, truly!"

She turned to go, then stopped. The dog's chain was rattling again.

This time, the dark figure I thought I'd seen before didn't slip into the shadows. It was stooping to the dog, making low murmuring noises.

"Be that thou, Blazing Scalp?" said Hester.

Again I felt that neck-freezing sensation.

What *was* this?

A witch's familiar?

But the reply was human enough.

"Aye, 'tis, Hester. Is all well?"

An older boy's voice, rather husky.

He began to lope toward us.

"Stay!" said Hester. "I will join you now."

He seemed to *dissolve* to a standstill.

He was tall, without a hat, or so it seemed in that dim moonlight. About fifteen or sixteen, judging from his voice.

He put a protective arm around Hester as they went back along the dirt road.

"Sounds like he might be an Indian," murmured Willie. "A name like that."

"He acts like one," said Brains.

"If he is," said Wanda, "it's no wonder she's suspected of being a witch."

"Why?" asked McGurk.

"Well, people at that time—uh, *this* time—used to think of Indians as the 'Devil's imps.' "

"Maybe—" Mari began.

The dog had started to growl again and McGurk said, "Come on, men! We don't have any time to waste."

He knocked on the door. A sturdy middle-aged woman with a stern but pleasant face opened it.

"We've called to see Mistress Brown, ma'am," said McGurk. "I think she might be expecting us."

The woman stared.

"Wherever on earth—where have *you* come from?"

"Who is it, Nell?" came an old cracked voice.

"Some—some children, mistress!"

"Ask them to come in, then!" said the old woman.

Then, when we did: "Heh! heh! So they do, Nell, so they do look strange!"

The frail old figure had been standing at an open door at the far end of the kitchen. Then her white cap bobbed out of sight and her voice came drifting back: "But bring them in here. These are old friends of mine."

We looked at each other as Nell showed us into the old lady's room, muttering. "Well, you *are* honored, though I cannot think why!"

The tiny figure was back in the chair. Our hostess looked much more alert now.

"Very, *very* old friends!" she said, with a cackle of glee. "Come in, Sir Jack, Sir Joey and—bless me—Lady Wanda and Lady Mari! Come in! You too, Sir Willie! Do not look so affrighted. *And* you, Master Brains!"

$\mathbb{6}$ One Half of a Dragon

I think we *all* must have looked pretty scared by now. Being addressed by the names we were known as only on our first trip, to medieval Britain! And by a woman who looked so *ancient*! In the light from the oil lamp and the flickering fire, her face was a mass of wrinkles and her eyes were two small, shining buttons. We'd never met anyone like that on our first trip. And that had been back in 1175, and this was 1692. She couldn't possibly have been *that* old, could she?

Then her mouth gave me the clue. Wide and smiling, with a long upper lip. A smile so broad it made her face go pear-shaped. A mouth with few teeth left, if any, but yes, of course—

"Gwyneth!" I gasped. "Gwyneth Owen!"

She cackled, then coughed.

"Aye! 'Tis I, Joey!" she wheezed. "All that is left of me. . . ."

The others had been doing some gasping, too. I mean, she'd been fourteen when we'd last seen her and her twin brother, Gareth. We'd met them at the castle, where they'd been prisoners of Melisande the Bad. The princess had made them dress up in a dragon outfit to lure knights into her ambush. I smiled at the thought of Hester calling her "somewhat of a dragon." Somewhat? She'd been exactly one half of a dragon!

"Did—did you get back to your correct century, after all?" said McGurk.

Gareth and Gwyneth had been time travelers, too. They'd come from the year 1610. *They* didn't have walkie-talkies, of course. They'd traveled on a mixture of strange herbs they'd accidentally drunk.

"Aye," wheezed the old lady. "After you had gone. . . . We were employed by King Henry. . . . Gareth, a page; I, a lady's maid . . . but he had a wonderful herb garden. . . . 'Twas there we found the exact mixture . . . for the potion we needed . . . to transport us back."

She paused, clutching her chest.

"Take it easy, ma'am," said Wanda.

Mistress Brown waved her away.

" 'Tis all right, child. . . . I am . . . just a little weak. . . . But seeing you all, it has taken fifty years off me. I am ninety-six now. . . . The oldest woman hereabouts . . ."

She seemed to have gotten her second wind. She went on to tell us:

1. How she and Gareth came over from England in 1630.

2. How she'd been married to a man called Edward Brown, who died on the voyage.

3. How she'd never been able to have any kids of her own.

4. How she and Gareth had worked hard and how she now owned the biggest tract of land in the township.

"What about Gareth?" McGurk asked, during a pause.

"He died years ago . . . when he was sixty-five . . . God rest his soul. . . . But I have not had a minute's loneliness."

Then she told us about all the waifs and strays she'd welcomed and treated like children of her own. Orphans, mostly, whose parents had either died from disease or been killed by Indians.

"Heh! heh! And not only children," she said. "Once we gave refuge to a judge from England. . . . Wanted by King Charles the Second . . . because he had been one of the judges . . . that had condemned his father to death. . . . John Dixwell, his name was . . . but he changed it to James Davids."

It was then that McGurk murmured, "Fugitives often do that."

Whether it was out of politeness, to give our old

friend's tongue a rest, or he did it to break up her flow of chatter, I'm not sure. I mean we *were* here on a mission.

It worked, anyway.

"Eh?" she gasped, lying farther back. "Fugitives?"

"Yes, ma'am. They often use the same intitials for their assumed names. Like J. D. for John Dixwell *or* James Davids."

"Oh . . . yes . . ." she murmured. But it was easy to tell she'd lost the thread. Which gave McGurk his chance.

"Mistress Brown—" he began.

"Gwyneth," she said.

"Gwyneth," said McGurk, "we are here on an urgent mission. Hester Bidgood—"

The old lady sat up.

"Aye, poor child! . . . I fear she is in some danger. . . . And . . . and I suspect 'tis on my account!"

"Oh?"

"Yes. She is a goddaughter of mine. . . . An orphan. . . . Lives with her aunt on my land. . . . There are those in this town who have . . . who have coveted my land ever since Gareth's death. . . . They wish me to sell it to them. . . . And because I won't, I fear they might persecute her. . . . Knowing she is my favorite. . . . One man in particular—"

There was the sound of knocking. The old lady tilted

her head to one side. A flicker of fear crossed her face when she heard the muffled sound of voices—Nell's and a man's.

Then Nell came in.

" 'Tis himself again. Mr. Peabody—"

"Talk of the Devil!" gasped the old lady.

"He wishes to know if you have thought over his latest offer."

"Tell him no!" said Mistress Brown. "And tell him . . . tell him I have visitors. . . . I cannot see him now."

"I do not think he expects you to, Mistress. He says if you have no answer for him tonight, mayhap you will do him the honor of attending his Thursday lecture tomorrow. He says you may hear that which will help to change your mind."

The bundle of shawls quivered.

"Fiddlesticks!" Mistress Brown broke off, coughing. "But wait—yes. . . . I might just afford him that honor. Yes! . . . Heh! . . . Yes, indeed! . . . And I will bring my guests, too." She turned and, lowering her voice, said, " 'Twill be an opportunity for you to size him up. . . . For I fear that Jacob Peabody is your real adversary on this mission."

After Nell had left, our hostess suddenly looked alarmed.

"Do you think he saw you coming here?"

We looked at each other.

"I doubt it," said McGurk. "Why? What if he did?"

"Those clothes . . ." wheezed Gwyneth (because it *was* the Gwyneth part of Mistress Brown who answered). "We might be able to fool the rest of the towns-folk . . . who never travel anywhere . . . to fool them into believing these are the latest fashions in Virginia. . . . But Jacob Peabody is a man of the world. . . . He would know better."

"So what should we—?" Wanda began.

"But do not worry," said Gwyneth-in-Mistress-Brown. "If he has not seen you already . . . you will be in regular seventeenth-century clothes when he does. . . . I have a stock upstairs. . . . You will not be the first waifs I have given shelter to, believe me!" Then she threw up her feeble arms. "And Lord bless us! What am I thinking of? You must be starving. . . . And tired. . . ." She was drooping again now. "Though not as tired as I. . . . So you must . . . excuse me." She lifted her head. "Nell!" she called out faintly.

Nell came in at once.

I suspected she'd been listening at the keyhole.

7 The Six New Pilgrims

After we'd eaten (a delicious stew with rabbit and pork and beans and fresh cider to drink), Nell took us upstairs to what she called our "quarters." This was a long, low attic room with overhead beams and a stone chimney stack coming up through the middle, roughly dividing the room into two sections. There was a peculiar smell, which Willie identified as a mixture of woodsmoke, apples, and lavender.

Furniture: practically nil. There was a pile of thin straw mattresses, which reminded me of the castle. But here there was nothing on the floor, just plain bare boards, and no truckle beds like at the castle.

Wanda murmured something about "next time we better bring our sleeping bags"—and McGurk had to warn her with a scowl that we weren't alone.

"Plenty of blankets," said Nell, opening one of the chests that were lined up against the wall and letting out a powerful extra gust of dried lavender.

They looked very rough and hairy. But it was an improvement on the castle's old burlap sacking stuff, I guessed.

"There are more in the other chests," said Nell. "Where you will also find all the clothes you need. Be careful with the candles, the roof is of thatch."

She left us then, as if she felt uncomfortable around us in our modern clothes.

Well—she couldn't have felt half as uncomfortable as *we* did in her seventeenth-century gear! Us guys, anyway.

I mean it's all right for girls. They *like* dressing up. And they're used to wearing long dresses, at least occasionally.

So *we* didn't laugh much when Mari and Wanda came back from around the chimney stack in their white caps and long dresses and big collars and aprons, or stomachers, or whatever they called them.

But when it was the guys' turn, that was different.

I mean, okay. The headgear wasn't all that different from what we knew already: the two high-crowned hats McGurk and I picked and the woollen stocking caps the others chose. But the rest of the stuff—!

Like:

Long woollen stockings that went to the top of our legs.

Knee breeches—with *ribbons* at the bottom.

Rough leather shoes with leather laces, which weren't

bad, I suppose, but somehow clumsy feeling. (Ms. Ellis hadn't prepared us for the fact that there were no ready-made right or left shoes in those days. Just straight-on-down-the-middle shoes that you were supposed to *wear* into shape.)

The girls had to prop each other up, they laughed so much as we hobbled about. And although this made some of us mad (especially Brains, whose knee breeches came almost down to his ankles, the nearest fit he could find)—we, too, couldn't help laughing when we looked at each other.

Finally, McGurk said, "Cut it out, men, and let's get on task. Line up while I check you out."

Even then we didn't stop right away, and we giggled at him, standing there so serious, looking us up and down with such a fierce scowl.

"I said cut it out!" he growled. "This might make all the difference between blending into the background or getting accused of being witches ourselves. . . .

"Like *you*, Officer Bellingham. Take off that watch and stash it with your regular clothes. . . .

"You too, Officer Yoshimura. Get those Reeboks changed. Your dress isn't that long and I can see them from here."

"What about their glasses, Chief McGurk?" said Mari, looking a bit miffed with herself at having to be repri-manded.

"I can't see without *mine!*" Brains protested.

"Me either," I said. "Anyway, it isn't like back in the twelfth century. Glasses *have* been invented by *now.* They look clumsier and cruder, sure, and there aren't many. But let's hope they'll think ours are the latest fashion in Virginia. Even the Peabody guy won't be so sure."

"Huh!" grunted McGurk. "Well, try not to let anyone inspect them too closely. . . . And by the way, Officer Rockaway, I notice you've got your notebook and pen with you this trip. Keep *them* out of sight."

"I've already decided that," I said. "I intend to leave them here when we go out and write up the notes when we get back here."

That reminded me of Hester's casebook.

"In fact I'm going to be making some notes tonight."

McGurk flashed me a keen look.

"What about?"

I told him.

And that's when they *all* got serious, sitting down on the chests or mattresses, like it was a regular HQ case conference.

"We're gonna have to find out more about this Peabody guy, men," said McGurk, after I'd told them what I'd managed to read.

"We'll get a good chance to do that at the lecture tomorrow," said Wanda.

"Sure," said McGurk. "But what I have in mind is questioning Hester Bidgood. Asking her just *what* she has on Peabody. *And* about that mysterious guest of his."

All this time, he was absentmindedly scratching himself—legs, body, arms, neck. The rest of us were doing some scratching, too. We were so engrossed in our plans, *we* weren't fully conscious of it, either.

But, boy, what with that coarse clothing and the fact that one thing they definitely *hadn't* invented by the seventeenth century was insecticide, we were in for one very itchy time!

I'll not mention it again. But you can take it from me that whatever we were doing—quietly investigating or running for our lives or holding villains at bay—we were also doing some scratching.

I mean, this is a part of a page of notes I made that evening:

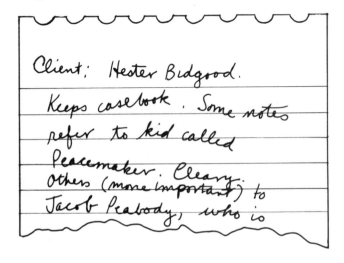

Client: Hester Bidgood.
Keeps casebook. Some notes
refer to kid called
Peacemaker. Cleary.
Others (more important) to
Jacob Peabody, who is

It wasn't only the bad light that made the lines go up and down. No sir. It was the itching. . . .

"Okay, men," said McGurk, finally. "We have to be on our toes tomorrow. One hundred percent alert. So let's hit the sack."

Well, tired though I was, it was some time before I dropped off to sleep. My mind was too busy, thinking about Hester and her plight and the shadow she called Blazing Scalp and Jacob Peabody and, most of all, Mistress Gwyneth Brown. I just couldn't get over the contrast between the way she looked now and the bright young girl we'd met only a few weeks ago.

Would we all get like that one day? I wondered.

But no, I told myself. Impossible.

In a few years, according to Brains, scientists would invent a pill which would make us live forever and never grow old and . . .

At that point, I must have fallen asleep. Which was a good thing. Because McGurk was right. The next day we certainly did have to be on our toes. One *thousand* percent alert, in fact.

After all, it was the day Jacob Peabody officially announced the start of the open season for hunting witches in our part of the world!

8 Jacob Peabody

Hey, I'm sorry!

There's very little known about seventeenth-century townships deep inside New England. People didn't write much about their surroundings. They were too busy clearing and digging and planting and trapping and fighting off wolves and bears and Indians and burying their dead and praying and preaching. In fact, I think maybe listening to preaching was the lighter side of things, like their "TV."

So all right. As Recorder of the McGurk Organization, I had a great opportunity to fill in those gaps.

But we were there to rescue an innocent kid. And to try to put a stop to the scheming of a real, true, double-dyed, stick-at-nothing, big-time villain. And when you come eyeball to eyeball with one of *them*—believe me— you quickly forget about the old-fashioned customs and looks of a place. You take care never—but never—to take your attention off a guy like that, if you wish to stay in one piece.

I know *I* won't ever forget the exact look in Jacob Peabody's eyes when he gave the Thursday lecture that morning!

However, before we get into that, I will tell you one thing that struck us as we went here and there during the next few days. It was how Wanda had managed to give a good general impression of the place pictorially. That was when Ms. Ellis got her to make a sketch of what it must have looked like, based on that map she'd drawn.

So here it is, as a crow (or a witch!) might have seen it, flying in from the south on that golden fall morning in 1692—just before all hell broke loose:

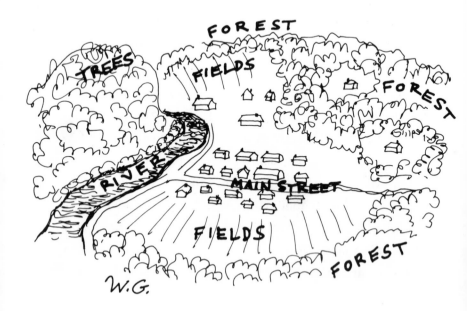

And now, about Jacob Peabody's lecture and those eyes of his . . .

Well, Mistress Brown went on ahead of us in a two-wheeled cart pulled by a pony and driven by one of her hired hands. We ourselves walked to the Meeting House with Nell, in twos. She seemed much more comfortable around us now that we were wearing the old borrowed clothes. I was paired with McGurk up front, and she kept up a commentary all the way.

"That is where Hester lives with her aunt, Goody Bidgood, in that little house yonder. And that is Rob MacGregor hastening to join them . . . though why Goody Bidgood allows such familiarity, I do not know, and him a half Injun and all. . . .

"And this is where Mr. Luke Lawson lives. One of Mistress Brown's godchilder. He's a growed man now and a magistrate hisself. And acrosst there is the minister's house, the Reverend Mr. Phipps. A fine, God-fearin' man, but 'tis a weak one and a poor speaker. I am right glad *he* is not giving the lecture. . . .

"Good morning, Goody Hurst.

"A pleasant and fruitful day to ye, Mr. Pringle."

We were now in the Main Street, with other people all heading in the same direction. We were getting plenty of curious glances, but Nell didn't stop to introduce us. Not that they'd have stopped to listen, anyway. They all

seemed much too concerned to get to the meeting, looking sort of anxious, yet eager. And scared, too, I guess.

"And that acrosst the street," Nell was continuing,
"that be the ordinary, what you might call *tavern,* con-
ducted by Ezra Cleary. He also keeps the jail, and God
grant you never go inside of either. That is he now and
his wife."

She had nodded toward a fat, oily-faced man, with an
even fatter woman with mean little eyes. They were just
closing the tavern door. There was a boy between them,
a scrawny kid about our age, with dirty-looking yellow
hair. He had bulging eyes, like Hester's. They were
bulging now, anyway, as he stared at us.

"That with them is their son, Peacemaker," Nell was
saying, "who rightly shoulda been called Troublemaker.
Which he is, except for when he is too busy running
errands for his father and Jacob Peabody."

"Is *he* anywhere about?" asked McGurk. "Jacob Peabody?"

"Nay. He will already be inside the Meeting House,
in the vestry, preparing for his lecture. Preening before
a mirror, I would not doubt, for 'tis a vain man, very.
And this long, gangly, squinting man with the scrawny,
ill-visaged goodwife is Zeke Cleary, our town crier and
one of the marshalls. Ezra's brother and a bad farmer.
They are a worthless family. . . ."

Then Nell fell silent as we took off our hats and went inside to join Gwyneth, who was already sitting on the front pew. She was wrapped in more shawls than ever and propped up with cushions. She waved impatiently for us to come sit down in the space at her side.

I looked around. Hester and her aunt and the youth Nell had called Rob MacGregor were just taking their places near the back. Rob didn't look much like an Indian then, in his dark blue regular clothes and the tall hat he was holding like a shield. In fact, *his* hair was red, too, though a darker shade than Hester's or McGurk's. It was shorter than most of the other males'—especially at the sides—and sort of spiky and unruly at the top, like Brains's would be if he ever let it grow. But that was the only unusual thing about his looks.

"Why do you say he's half Indian, Nell?" I asked.

But now she was tight-lipped again and seemed not to hear. Then I heard McGurk murmur, "This looks like Jacob Peabody now," and there was a general hush as the man stepped toward the rough platform.

Well, at *first* he looked harmless enough—a tall, heavily built man in neat, black clothes. But they were a rich black, not rusty black like some of the others', and he wore stockings that seemed to be made of silk. Also, a big, white collar that really sparkled. I mean, all in all, he seemed to *ooze* with wealth and comfortable living.

But his eyes . . . Boy, there was nothing comfortable about *them*! Dark and glowing under bushy black eyebrows, they slowly swept the audience. It seemed to me they glowed a little brighter when they came to Mistress Brown, but they didn't linger. And their survey didn't stop until they fell on Peacemaker Cleary just behind us.

Jacob Peabody frowned slightly and beckoned.

Peacemaker Cleary went up to him looking a bit guarded, ready to duck, and I don't blame him, because with a guy like Peabody you never know. But the man's expression was bland enough as he bent to the boy and said something in a very low voice.

Peacemaker listened and nodded and relaxed in a squirmy way. He even managed a pleasant smile (if you could call the ugly, lopsided leer pleasant) just before he turned and went away. Not to his place, though, but to the back and out through the door.

"A herrand," I heard his mother whisper importantly.

Jacob Peabody was now standing erect on the platform, one hand behind his back, the other on the desk, with the thunderclouds gathering behind those black brows. Then: "The text for this my lecture today," he rumbled, "I take from the book of Exodus, chapter 22, verse 18. . . ."

There was a rustle went around like the stirring of snakes under dead leaves. A rustle of expectation, I guessed. Expectation *and* recognition, even before he read that verse out in a low, purring, but very chilling voice.

" *'Thou shalt not suffer a witch to live.'* "

Dead silence.

"You know me for a plain-speaking man, my friends," he continued, after a few moments. "But nothing *I* say could be plainer than that. . . .

" *'Thou*—shalt *not*—suffer a *witch*—to *live. . . .'* "

Another deathly silence. They all seemed to be holding their breath.

Then they relaxed some (it came out like a faint sigh, the first whisper of a hurricane) as he went on in a gentler tone.

"I have quoted this before, as you all know." Then, with a sudden flash of the eyes and teeth he was thundering once more. *"And I shall be quoting it again and again and again!"* Then, softer: "Because know ye this. There be witches busy with their Satanic Master's evil work even now—even as I speak—in this colony of ours, as well as in that other colony to the north. . . .

"Let me remind you of these things. . . ."

He began to speak of the witchcraft trials and confessions and hangings that had been taking place up in Massachusetts—in Salem and in Andover. He lingered—I thought lovingly and gloatingly—over some of the things those so-called witches were supposed to have done, and his audience seemed to be drinking it all in. I even found myself beginning to wonder if, after all, some of those witch-hunters had been right. And then I realized it was because of his voice and his eyes: the singsong rise and fall of the sentences, the slow, piercing looks he swept across us.

At my side, I could hear McGurk grunting and shuffling with angry disagreement, but there were times when even he became still and silent, with a half-open mouth.

I also heard:

1. A faint, eerie echo of Peabody's words from time to time—a *very* creepy echo, until I realized it was Mari, unconsciously practicing one of her skills, spellbound into imitating this strange, compelling voice, if only in whispers.

2. Willie's breathing rasping through his nose, getting quicker and harsher at the more bloodcurdling bits.

3. A couple of isolated, muttered comments of Brains's that sounded like, "Baloney! Totally unscientific!" and "No such thing!"—both of which froze in his throat as the sweep of those eyes ranged closer.

4. Wanda, stifling a groan.

Then the voice became brisker and more menacing.

"But ask not if all this is far off and has naught to do with us. Only recollect. How many seemingly unexplainable things have happened and are happening daily in this our own community? Babes that suddenly sicken and die for no apparent reason. Hale and hearty men who sustain the merest scratch and who, before the next moon has waxed and waned, have died horrible deaths, chattering like fiends, their limbs twitching and prinking as in some obscene dance—listening to music that is only to be heard by them. . . ."

And so on, citing cows that stopped giving milk, dogs that suddenly went mad, swarms of bees that turned on people who'd been nowhere near them.

"And whose work *is* this, think you—eh? Whose? Whose?"

"The Devil's!" screeched a woman in a strangled voice—and I think it was Mrs. Zeke Cleary.

"True," purred Peabody, "true, true. But who is it that does the Devil's work for him, ministers to him at dead of night and in the depths of the forest?"

He leaned forward.

"Who but his *witches*?"

He stood up straight again.

"Oh, yes, friends! We have not been spared the infestation. There are strangers in our midst!"

Suddenly, I was aware that scores of eyes had swiveled our way.

"Uh-oh," I heard Wanda gasp.

But we needn't have worried. Not right then, anyway. Peabody himself was coming to our rescue.

"No, friends!" he rumbled. "I refer not to innocent strangers, those who come from afar. I refer to those who have dwelt among us all their lives. Whom we think we know, but whom we know not at all. Because *they* are the strangers, both in spirit and in their very souls. *They* are the ones who have had (and still do have) dark dealings with the Devil."

An angry murmur began to arise. Peabody seemed to like its sound. His eyes glowed brighter, his voice sank deeper.

"*They* are the real strangers! And it is our duty—nay, our sacred obligation—*to seek them out and flush them out!*" (His voice was rising now, and flecks of frothy spittle flew from his lips.) "To—to destroy them root and branch!" he bellowed. "Before they destroy *us*!"

Then he sat down suddenly on a chair behind the desk and sank his head on his hand.

In the dead silence that followed, Mr. Phipps, the man Nell had pointed out as the minister, a guy with a face like a sick and frightened turkey's, got up and said a short prayer.

His voice was soft and soothing compared to Peabody's. But when he'd finished, the "amens" quickly grew to a rumble—a surging, rattling rumble like a breaker crashing down on a shingly beach.

At the side of the minister, Jacob Peabody's head rose slightly from behind the hands that he'd been clasping in prayer. *His* eyes were shining with triumph as they opened and ranged across the scared and angry faces before finally coming to rest on Mistress Brown's.

It was only for a moment, but it was enough.

"Nell," she said, in a low, trembling voice, "we must get back as speedily as possible! *All* of us!"

$\textcircled{9}$ The Knife of Many Uses

But the journey back wasn't as speedy as Mistress Brown had hoped.

When we got into the street, the townspeople were already gathering in little clusters. Their faces still had that grave but excited look. They were obviously discussing Peabody's lecture.

They weren't taking any special notice of us, but they were making it difficult for us to walk quickly in our pairs. Before we'd gone many yards, we'd sort of bunched up, with Nell forging ahead, using her bulk to push past people standing in her way.

She seemed to have forgotten about us.

And then we saw why.

About halfway down the street, there was another, larger bunch of people. In the middle, head and shoulders above them, was Mistress Brown, looking frightened but fierce.

"Oh, no!" murmured Wanda. "I hope they haven't started on *her*!"

But it wasn't because Mistress Brown had been put on a platform, to be pilloried or something even worse. She was still sitting in her cart.

"What is happening?" said Nell. "Mistress, are you all right?"

" 'Tis nothing, Nell," said our hostess, still looking tense even so. "Paddy hath a pebble in his shoe."

"Aye, Nell," said Martin, the hired man. "Hold him, would ye, while I pry it loose."

" 'Tis an omen!" a woman growled, shaking her head. "A sign."

"Think you so?" said the man with her. "A sign of what?"

"Nay!" said the woman, in a suddenly guarded voice. "Mayhap she has been bewitched."

"Bewitched? Mistress Brown?"

"Aye. Why not? You heard Mr. Peabody. They respect neither the rich nor the poor. . . ."

I guess in those days even *talk* of witches could be dangerous. I mean, one minute you could be pointed out as being bewitched, and the next, you could be accused of witchcraft.

Mistress Brown seemed to sense this.

"Hurry, Martin!" she said.

" 'Tis very tight, mistress," said the man, stabbing away with the tip of a knife.

"I hope he knows what he's doing," murmured Wanda. "One slip and that animal might bolt!"

Then suddenly a new voice arose.

"Hey! Why don't I use this?"

Brains's.

He was digging into the pockets of his oversize breeches.

"You dummy!" growled McGurk, as Brains's hand emerged with something red and shiny in it. "What d'you think you're doing, Officer Bellingham?"

Brains blinked.

"This!" he said, plucking at his Swiss Army knife. He pulled out the corkscrew in his haste, then the glass cutter, before finding the one he wanted. "For getting pebbles out of horse's hooves. I've always wanted the chance to use it for real. And now—"

"Put it away! Didn't you hear what I told you last night?"

McGurk's eyes were flitting frantically from side to side. Luckily, most of the bystanders were too busy watching the gasping, straining, jabbing Martin, or Nell as she whispered anxiously in Paddy's ear, or Mistress Brown, who had closed her eyes and seemed to be praying.

Brains's face flushed.

"Oh, gosh! I—I'm sorry, McGurk! I—I—"

He seemed to be all fingers and thumbs as he fumbled with the horse's hoof thing, trying to push it back.

Then he nearly dropped the knife when a voice behind him said: "Ho! What—what is *that*?"

It was Peacemaker Cleary. His greeny-gray eyes were popping as he stared at the slick, shiny red object, with its white cross and its corkscrew, which, in his confusion, Brains had somehow managed to pull out again.

Peacemaker's face was streaked with sweat, as if he'd been running. He had one hand inside his doublet, where there was a bulge, but his other was reaching out for the knife.

McGurk's hand beat his to it. Snatching the knife from Brains, he began to pluck out some of the implements himself.

" 'Tis only a knife of many uses," he said, in a half-bored voice. (Actually, he was having eggs, as he told us later: "I mean, I knew if we made too much of a fuss about concealing it, it would only double the jerk's suspicions.")

"Wh-where did you get it?" Peacemaker asked, still out of breath from his running.

"Back in Virginia," said McGurk, keeping up the nonchalant tone. "They sell them all over Virginia."

Now, McGurk was not telling a lie. After all, they *do* sell Swiss Army knives all over Virginia. *And* Nebraska *and* California. In every state in the Union, come to that. Nowadays. In the late twentieth century.

But Peacemaker was only thinking seventeenth century, of course.

"They do?" he said.

"Sure," said McGurk.

"Zooks!" said Peacemaker, still holding out a sticky-looking hand and wiggling his fingers. "Could I—?"

"Boy!"

The voice cracked across our backs like a whip.

It was Jacob Peabody's. His eyes looked stormy again under the tall, black hat. He was standing a little way from the crowd.

Peacemaker began to quiver.

"Yes, sir, Mr. Peabody, sir! I was just—"

"Why are you dawdling? Did I not charge you with an errand of the utmost urgency?"

"Y-yes, Mr. Peabody." Peacemaker's hand was groping about under his doublet. "I have it, sir. 'Twas where I—"

"Be quiet!" rumbled the man. "And bring it to me."

His gloomy eyes had lit up some.

"Yes, sir," said Peacemaker, trotting toward him and beginning to draw the object out.

"Not *here*, boy!" growled Peabody.

As they went away, Willie's nose quivered in a series of little, harsh sniffs.

"What is it, Officer Sandowsky?"

"Yes," murmured Willie, staring after the departing pair.

"What d'you mean—yes?"

"Him," said Willie. "That kid."

"Yeah," said Wanda, wrinkling her nose. "I caught it, too. I guess he doesn't wash often. And he did seem to be in a hurry, sweating and—"

"No, not that!" said Willie, looking like he resented an amateur muscling in on his expert territory. "*Besides* that. . . . A kind of—uh—piney, pitchy smell. Especially when he wiggled his fingers."

McGurk grunted.

"So what? Maybe that was his errand. Chopping firewood for Peabody. Maybe he—"

"McGurk . . ."

Brains's voice was polite.

"What?"

"May I have my Swiss—?"

"No! You may *not*, Officer Bellingham! And when we get back to base, men, I'm gonna have something to say about this!"

As he was speaking, a murmur went up from the crowd—a mixture of relief and something else I couldn't identify. Something much less pleasant, anyway. Maybe disappointment—an ugly thwarted kind of disappointment.

Martin was getting back in the driving seat, and Mistress Brown was settling back on her cushions, looking very pale.

"Come," said Nell, glancing anxiously at the faces of the bystanders. "There is no more time to be wasted. I fear my mistress is not well!"

10 Client in Distress

While Nell was undressing Mistress Brown and putting her to bed, McGurk gave *us* a dressing-down in the attic.

"I warned you about what might happen, men, and it did!" he concluded, looking grim. "So I'm going to confiscate Officer Bellingham's knife and anything else like that for the duration of the mission. All right? . . . So if you've been holding out on anything—give!"

I had a couple of dollars. Willie had a wad of gum, well chewed, wrapped in a handkerchief. Mari had a pack of throat lozenges. Brains added to his disgrace by confessing to a bunch of Band-Aids, claiming that as science expert, he never knew when he might have to give medical assistance in the field. And Wanda made a fuss about an elasticized headband which she swore couldn't be seen under her cap.

It didn't make any difference. Dollar bills, gum, throat

lozenges, Band-Aids, and headband, all had to be stashed in one of the chests.

Willie was looking worried.

"Do you think that Cleary kid suspects us now, McGurk?" he said. "On account of Brains's knife?"

"Yes," I said. "I've been wondering that. Did he really swallow it, about buying it in Virginia?"

"Well—" McGurk began. Then Mari broke in.

"Excuse me, Chief McGurk, but I think he *did* believe you. I was watching his face. He was just curious."

Mari is good at reading the faces of people when they are speaking, and McGurk respects that.

"Yes," he said. "I think you're right, Officer Yoshi-mura. But don't any of you think we can keep *on* getting away with it. We—"

There was the sound of a loud, urgent knocking coming from downstairs.

We listened and heard the door being opened.

"Oh, hello, Hester. Come in, child, you look—"

"Where are they, Nell?"

"Who?"

"The visitors, those who were with you at the meet-ing—"

"Why, I believe they are in the attic—"

Nell had hardly gotten the words out when the door burst open and Hester came in, capless, hair flying loose, eyes staring.

"*You!*" she said, heading straight for me. "You give me back my book! Right now! *You hear?*" she said, stamping and shaking the handful of my jacket she'd grabbed.

"But—but I haven't got your book!" I protested. "What book, anyway?"

Her eyes flashed.

" 'What book?'! *You* know what book! My book of causes, which you were so interesed in last night!"

"Hold it!" said McGurk, trying to come between us. "Hold it right there, miss! My officer does *not* have your book!"

She relaxed her grip.

"But—but it has gone! I went to get it and it has gone!"

The tears had started.

"Sit down," McGurk said, leading her to one of the chests. "Officer Grieg . . ." Wanda went and put an arm around the slumped shoulders. "Just take your time," McGurk went on, "and tell us about it. Where *was* it, anyway?"

"I—I had it in a s-secret place. In my hut . . ."

"What secret place?"

"In—among the logs. Four rows from the bottom, four logs to the right, then there were four short logs which—which left a cavity—and—it was there I kept it and now 'tis *gone!*"

The tears were falling in full spate now.

"Very neat idea," murmured Wanda, soothingly. "Like a safe with a combination lock."

"Wh-what?" Hester blinked up at her.

"Never mind that now!" said McGurk, frowning at Wanda. "When was the last time you put it there, Hester?"

"Last night. After you had been. I went back and—"

"Was that Blazing Scalp—uh—that Rob MacGregor with you when you stashed the book away?"

"Yes—I mean no. I mean he waited outside while—oh, dear! Oh, Lord! Who can have taken it?"

"When did you find out it had gone?"

"Just now. After the lecture, I went straight to the hut. The door was open. The lock had been forced."

McGurk was frowning, his eyes in slits.

"And there were logs all over the floor, right?"

Hester looked up, bewildered.

"No. Just those four short ones."

McGurk grunted.

"So the perpetrator knew just where to look, huh?"

"The perp—*what* purple traitor?"

"The thief, miss. Who else knew about the hiding place? I mean besides Rob—"

Hester stamped.

"I tell you not even *he* knew! I never ever took it out or put it back while anyone else was with me."

"Good thinking, miss. We detectives—uh—investigatours and investigatrixes—we can never be too careful. We—"

"*Hey!*"

It was Willie, snapping his fingers.

"What?" said McGurk.

He looked hopeful, because Willie was also twitching his nose.

"That Cleary kid!" said Willie. "That smell of pine pitch! He—"

"Of *course!*" said Wanda. "*That's* where he'd been! *That* was what Jacob Peabody had sent him for! Knowing Hester was safely in the Meeting House. *That's* what the jerk had under his jacket!" She swung back to the horrified Hester. "I bet those short logs were sticky with resin, weren't they, honey?"

But Hester was sobbing. She'd been looking from face to face with frightened eyes, and now she'd buried her own face in her pinafore.

"Oh, Lord, oh, Heavenly Father!" she began to moan, rocking back and forward. Then she suddenly looked up, tears streaming down her cheeks. "You—you really think my book is now in the hands of that—of Jacob Peabody?"

"I'm sure of it," said McGurk. He still looked puzzled, though. "But why would he be so keen to get hold of it?"

"Because—because he suspects—nay, he must *know*—that I have been investigating him. Peacemaker

Cleary must have been espying on me more than I had feared."

I remembered the dark figure that had been lurking outside the hut when we first arrived. Maybe that hadn't been Blazing Scalp, a.k.a. Rob MacGregor, after all.

"What kind of investigations?" McGurk was asking. "You can tell us in confidence. What has Jacob Peabody been up to?"

Hester shuddered.

"Many things. Evil Things. Things that would surely put *him* in jail. And—and even to the gallows. I have been compiling proof of these things and I—I was intending to—"

"Go on," murmured McGurk, looking more interested than ever.

"I was intending to add some of the inciteful words he spake in the lecture when I—when I found the lock broken."

"The lecture was connected with his—uh—evil deeds, then?"

"Oh, but surely."

McGurk waited, but she'd suddenly clammed up. He tried a new tack.

"Officer Rockaway here tells me he saw something in the book about a mysterious guest of Peabody's."

She cast me an apologetic glance.

"I am sorry, Officer—uh—"

"Joey," I said, "Joseph," I added, to make her feel more at home.

"I am sorry, Joseph, that I accused you unjustly."

"That's okay," I said, adding, " 'Tis nothing."

"This mysterious guest?" growled McGurk.

"Oh, yes . . . sorry. . . . He is part of Mr. Peabody's deadly plot, I am sure. And Rob thinks so, too. Rob is my helper in my investigations—"

"Your officer, yeah," said McGurk. "Like these guys are *my*—"

There was a thunderous knocking from below. Even louder and more insistent than Hester's had been.

We all froze.

Then we heard voices. A man's at first, saying something we couldn't make out, followed by Nell's, rising.

"No. You *cannot* come in now, sir! My mistress—"

"This is lawful business, woman!" (Mari mouthed the name "Jacob Peabody!") "We are come to arrest Hester Bidgood. We have reason to believe she is here."

Hester stifled a moan.

"Arrest her, sirs?" said Nell, sounding shocked. "But for what?"

"For being a practitioner of the black and hideous arts of witchcraft. Of which we have proof positive. Now stand aside!"

"No, sir!" Nell sounded very firm. "Not under this roof! Not while my mistress is so ill!"

This seemed to pull the man up.

"Ho! Ill, is she? You heard that, Cleary? . . . Very well, my good woman. *Then send the witch Bidgood out unto us now, or we shall force an entry whether your mistress be ill or not!*"

11 Hester's Flight

For once, McGurk was fresh out of ideas.

We'd been standing in a horror-stricken group. Almost unconsciously, we had followed McGurk's lead in placing ourselves between the door and our client.

She herself stood there white-faced, her head jerking this way and that. Then, as we heard Nell coming up the stairs, Hester turned to McGurk with a desperate, pleading look.

He shrugged lamely.

There was a tap on the door.

"Hester, my dear, Jacob Peabody wishes to see you." Nell sounded hesitant, hushed, reluctant. "I—I do not know what to tell them. They say—"

"Tell them," said McGurk, still looking around anxiously (stalling, as he confessed later, trying to figure out whether to attempt to hide Hester in one of the chests or to use the chests for barricading ourselves in).

"Tell them she won't be long. That she—that she's brushing her hair."

"But—" Nell began.

That was when there came the sound of a jay screech.

It seemed to galvanize Hester.

She ran to the window and flung it open.

We followed her.

The window looked out on the back of the house, on a ragged lawn and a few small apple trees and beyond them, some scrubby brush.

"I—I must fly!" gasped Hester, looking down. "Before 'tis too late!"

I moved closer, wondering whether she'd gone crazy with fear and now thought she really was a witch and could fly. Then I saw she was inspecting the ivy that grew right up to and around the window.

"Be careful, Hester," said Wanda, inspecting it herself. "It doesn't look strong enough to me."

"Yes," said McGurk, "listen to what Officer Grieg says. She's the climbing expert. There's no point in breaking your neck."

But Hester had already tucked up her skirts and had one leg out, testing for a foothold.

" 'Tis firm enough!" she muttered.

Then she was on her way down, the ivy swishing and swaying precariously.

And she nearly made it. But something gave about ten

feet from the ground, and she fell the rest of the way, landing on the grass in a sprawling heap. Thankfully, she didn't seem hurt.

As she picked herself up, Wanda gave a muffled cheer. "Good kid! She's done it! She's—"

But Hester hadn't been quick enough.

"Ha! Would you, you witch?!" bellowed Jacob Peabody, striding around the corner.

His two companions had already dashed between the fugitive and the scrub, cutting off her escape. Their muskets were now pointing at her.

She swung around and faced Peabody, just as Peacemaker Cleary came prancing around the corner.

"I see her, I see her!" he was screeching. "I see her fly down! I see her dark wings a-spreading and a-flapping! Just like last night—flying in my bedroom window she was—and him, too, *him*, lurking in they bushes. I see him ready to fly out, that Injun of hers—"

"Be quiet!" snapped Peabody. "We will deal with the others later. I fear there will be many more when she confesses."

"C-confesses?" stammered Hester. "To—to what, sir?"

"To being a witch, of course!" said Peabody.

"Aye! Witch, witch, witch!" screeched Peacemaker, doing a couple of somersaults on the grass. "And him, too, over there—"

"*Silence!*" thundered Peabody. He scowled down at Hester. "A witch who hath had dealings with the Devil!"

Then Nell came and made as if to put herself between Hester and her accuser.

"Stand back!" growled one of the men.

Nell stopped, but turned to Peabody.

"What proof have you for this?" she demanded.

Peabody's eyes glowed as, smirking, he reached into a pocket and brought out a piece of paper.

"Quite enough!" he said. "*This* is the proof. And in her own hand, too."

I couldn't see it clearly from up there, but I soon realized what it was. With its ragged, torn edge and Peabody's next words, it could only have been one thing.

" 'Hester Bidgood,' " Peabody read out, in a slow, sneering voice. " 'Investigatrix of Evill Deedes. Her Book.' " He looked up and shook it in her face. "Do you deny this, too, wench? Is this or is this not your hand?"

"My book!" gasped Hester. "My record of causes!"

"Ha!" bellowed Peabody, his face one big, ugly, triumphant leer. "So there is a book, too?" (Wanda stirred angrily. "He knows darn well there is!" she muttered. "Yes," murmured Mari, "he is lying. I can see by—" "Quiet, men!" whispered McGurk.)

Peabody was continuing: "A book of *records*, forsooth! Records of your transactions with the Dark One, no doubt. Mark that, Marshall Cleary," he said, turning to one of the men, whom I now recognized as Zeke Cleary, under the rusty steel helmet he was wearing. "And now to jail with her!"

He was carefully folding the paper, ready to stow it back in his pocket.

He nearly didn't make it. With a loud, chilling whoop, a figure bounded out of the bushes, heading straight for him.

It was Rob MacGregor, still in his meeting clothes, all set to snatch the "evidence" and make off with it, as we found out later.

But the whoop was his undoing. It startled the men, sure. But it gave them time to react.

When Rob was within a couple of paces from Peabody, Zeke Cleary swung the butt of the musket. It landed with a sickening crack and Rob pitched forward.

"Oh, Rob!" gasped Hester, beginning to stoop over his body. But the other marshall grabbed her arm and yanked her away.

Zeke Cleary himself bent over the unconscious youth.

"Shall we take him, too, sir?"

"Leave him!" Peabody snarled. "We will deal with that one in the Lord's good time. After we have extracted *her* testimony."

Then the three men went off, half dragging their moaning prisoner with them, with Peacemaker Cleary bringing up the rear, still doing an exultant cartwheel every few yards.

"I don't like the sound of *that!*" murmured Wanda. "*Extracting* her testimony. . . ."

"Never mind it now," said McGurk. "Let's go see what we can do to help Rob MacGregor. It looks like he could have croaked."

When we got down the stairs, we found Gwyneth, wrapped in a quilt, standing at the front door. She didn't seem to recognize us, as, swaying slightly, she addressed Nell in a quavering whisper.

"Send for Mr. Lawson, Nell. . . . And Mr. Phipps. Only *they* can—"

Then she fainted, falling into Nell's arms.

"Leave her with me," said Nell. "She is as light as a babe, poor soul. You go see to that poor lad."

But when we went out, the "poor lad" had gone. It was almost as if Rob hadn't rushed onto the scene at all—as if he'd been an apparition, the shade of the witch that Peacemaker Cleary had accused him of being.

Then: "Good thing he was still wearing his best clothes," McGurk muttered, going across to something lying on the grass, yards away. "It looks like this hat saved him from a fractured skull, men."

The high crown had a deep dent in it.

Then McGurk quickly pulled his hand away from the inside and stared at his fingers.

"Blood!" he gasped.

"I do hope he isn't *badly* injured!" said Wanda.

"So do I," growled McGurk. "With Hester in jail, we need all the help we can get. Especially from him."

12 Rob MacGregor

We searched the patch of scrub, but Rob was nowhere to be seen. Then Nell came out to join us, after making her mistress as comfortable as possible and sending one of the farmhands with the message to Mr. Lawson and Mr. Phipps.

"Mistress Brown is right," she said. "Only they can help Hester now. They and Rob Mac—Where is he?"

"Gone," said McGurk.

"Gone?"

"Vanished," said McGurk. "This is all that's left."

He held out the hat.

"Oh, woe worth the day!" Nell said, wringing her hands. Then she gripped them tight. "But—but he be very strong. The strongest lad of his age in the township, the way he has been reared."

"Being an Indian?" I said. "A half Indian?"

She sighed.

"Aye, God forgive me! I did say that. But I lied. 'Twas just that he was brought up by them, poor lad. Ever since he was six, when they killed his mother and father and made off with him."

"They—they let him live?" said Willie.

"For sure. They turned him into a regular savage brave and kep' him until he was about fourteen. Then he was sent back. Some sort of treaty, ransom, I know not."

"Wow!" gasped Wanda.

"Oh, it has happened to others, you know," said Nell. She looked at us curiously. "Doth this not happen sometimes in Virginia? Was none of you never captured by savages there?"

We murmured our no's. Mostly with relief in our voices. Except for McGurk. There was a tinge of envy in his.

"Are you sure he isn't called Mc*Gurk*?" he asked.

"Nay," said Nell. " 'Tis Mac*Gregor*."

"McGurk!" said Wanda. "Everyone with red hair and freckles doesn't have to be one of your ancest—uh—relations!"

"Well," muttered McGurk. "You never know. . . . But go on, Nell. About him being strong . . ."

"Aye. He is *that*. And skilled in all Injun things. Running, hunting, swimming. . . . A mighty powerful swimmer—Blazing *Beaver*, I woulda called him." Then Nell frowned. "But I fear 'tis in learned lawyer things that Hester needs most help right now. And Mr. Lawson, though he be a magistrate . . ."

She shook her head.

"I suppose Rob can't even *read*," murmured Wanda. Nell's eyebrows went up.

"Oh, but he can! Oh yes, he can *read*! Thanks be to Hester." She sighed. "When he come to live with his grandparents—still with his wild, spiky Injun topknot of hair and shy as a young colt—he was very backward in his regular schooling. Even just ordinary English speaking. Goody MacGregor tried to get him to go to school, but schoolteacher would have naught of him. Feared he might injure the small ones, if they should mock him. Which they woulda, you may be sure."

"So Hester—" Wanda began.

"She took pity on him, yes," said Nell. "Bless the child! And she learned him all she knew, which was much, for 'tis a clever girl she is."

"He was very lucky!" said Mari, gravely.

"Very," said Nell. "And he knows it. You never seen such gratitude. Worships her now. Follows her everywhere. Which has set some tongues wagging, even mine, but God forgive me—*'tis* gratitude and nothing worse. Just his desire to help and protect her for all she done for him."

I was beginning to like Nell more and more. When I first suspected her of snooping, listening through the keyhole, I was being unjust, I guess. Probably she *had* been eavesdropping. But only to make sure we hadn't come to do her beloved mistress any harm.

But McGurk's mind was on more urgent matters.

"Well, even if Rob can't help her now in a legal way, maybe he could help us to help her *escape*."

"Oh, that, aye!" said Nell. "If anyone can, he can. But—"

"So where will he be now, do you think?" said McGurk.

Nell shook her head.

"The Good Lord only knows. Trying to keep track of what is happening to Hester, you may be sure."

"At the jail?" said Wanda. "But they'll arrest him, too!"

"Well, maybe not right now will he go there," said Nell. "Most like he will wait for darkness."

"So meanwhile, he'll be holing up someplace," murmured McGurk.

"Yes, but where?" I said, thinking of the miles and miles of surrounding trees.

"What about his grandparents' place?" said Brains.

"I doubt he will a gone there," said Nell. " 'Twill be the first place Jacob Peabody will look when they bethink them to take him."

"Does he have a hideout?" asked McGurk. "Some den where he goes when he wants to be quiet and—well—go back to living like an Indian for a while?"

Nell's eyes widened.

"Why, yes. Hester has spoken of such a place. Nothing detailed, mind. Just that it is somewhere in the forest beyond the south fields."

"Huh!" grunted McGurk. "That still leaves thousands and thousands of acres of trees and—"

"Excuse me, Chief McGurk," said Mari. "I have a hunch."

McGurk frowned. Hunches are *his* expert territory.

"Well, Officer Yoshimura?"

"I have a hunch that if we go into the forest to the south—any part of it—*we* won't have to find Rob. He will find *us!*"

"Hey! Good thinking, Officer Yoshimura!" said McGurk. "Come on, men!"

"But you have not had any dinner!" said Nell.

"Later, Nell," he said. "First things first!"

13 Jacob Peabody's "Evill Deedes"

About two hours later, just when I was beginning to wish we'd listened to Nell and not Mari, he appeared.

I thought at first it was a mirage, brought on by hunger. I mean, one second there was this empty forest path, speckled and dancing with sunlight, and the next second there *he* was, a few yards ahead, speckled with sunlight himself.

"Oh!" gasped Wanda. "Rob?"

Instead of the knee breeches and heavy shoes, he was now wearing fringed leather leggings and moccasins. He had a loose, gray shirt and a stocking cap. His top half looked English (or Scottish, I guess), but down below his belt he was all Indian. In the belt was a sheathed hunting knife.

"I was *wondering* if you would come seeking me," he

said, sounding doubtful about whether he was glad to see us or not.

"Yeah," said McGurk. "How's the head?"

"Huh?"

"Where they hit you."

Rob gingerly touched the back of his cap.

" 'Tis healing. Just a split in the skin."

"I had something that would have helped that," said Brains, giving McGurk a reproachful look.

"Thank 'ee," said Rob. "But 'tis not necessary. I have applied some herbs."

"We have your hat back at Mistress Brown's place," said McGurk.

"Ah, good!" said Rob. He suddenly looked grim. "Please keep it for me. I will not be needing it for some days."

"Sure," murmured McGurk.

There was an awkward silence. Rob was carrying a fringed leather bag with a shoulder strap. It was bulging. He fumbled about like he was shifting it into a more comfortable position. I think he was really playing for time, sizing us up.

"We've come to help Hester," said Wanda. "If—if we can."

"Good," said Rob. "Do you—'" He paused, looking very worried. "Any news of her?"

"No, not really," said McGurk. "Mistress Brown has sent for Mr. Lawson and Mr. Phipps."

"Oh . . . *them!*" Rob muttered. "And what do they say?"

"We don't know," said McGurk. "We left before they arrived."

Rob shrugged.

"Well, let us hope," he said. "But in the meantime— pray, come with me."

He led us a few hundred yards along the path. He walked in long, loping strides. It brought us out to a large open space where the ground fell away and became swampy.

At the edge, near us, was a bushy speckled alder (at least that's what Wanda said it was, later). It still had lots of yellowish-brown leaves. Rob sat down cross-legged in the shade and motioned us to sit near him.

So we did, wondering what was coming next and gazing out across the swamp.

It was a very peaceful spot. The sky was a deep, cloudless blue, and the sun glinted here and there on patches of water between the reeds. Dotted among the reeds were clumps of undergrowth, like small islands, with a slightly bigger one out in the middle. From the far side, before the trees began again, I heard the tinkling sound of a stream.

Finally, Rob grunted and opened the bag.

"Walnuts," he said. "Would you like some?"

Boy, would we?!

"Don't grab!" said McGurk.

"There are plenty," said Rob. "Wait and I will open them with my knife."

He did this neatly and swiftly, handing them out as he shelled them, Wanda and Mari first.

We munched in silence. And this time there was nothing awkward about the silence. It was businesslike. *I've* never tasted walnuts so sweet and yummy!

After a while, we slowed down. Wanda was probing her teeth with the tip of her tongue. A small frown had crossed her face, and I was wondering if she'd lost a filling or something when she said, "Strange!"

"What is?" said McGurk.

"That fir branch over there, in the swamp. And there, a bit nearer, that's a branch of cedar, unless I'm very much mistaken. I wonder where *they* came from?"

Rob was looking at Wanda with great respect in his eyes.

"Huh . . . blown there," he murmured. "Big storm. Last week."

"We haven't come here on a nature trail, Officer Grieg!" McGurk said. He turned to Rob. "One way you *can* help Hester—"

"Yes?" said Rob, eagerly.

"About the book," said McGurk. "The book we now know that Jacob Peabody had that jerk Peacemaker Cleary steal for him."

"Ah, that!" said Rob. "You know about that?"

"Yes," said McGurk. "My officer—my friend Joseph here—says there were notes in it. About Peabody . . ."

"I only had time to *glance* through it," I said.

Rob was looking excited now, his brown eyes flashing.

"Yes, well, in it Hester wrote about the law *he* broke. He, Jacob Peabody. In the chapter in the Bible next to the one where it said about not suffering a witch to live. The one before it. Twenty-one. Verse 15. It says . . ."

He quoted it exactly. I looked it up later, and this is the one:

altar, that he may die.
¶15 And he that smiteth his father, or his mother, shall surely be put to death.
¶16 And he that

"Can this be proved?" said McGurk.

"Ah, well—'twas like this. Hester found an old servant woman who had been with the Peabody family. She told Hester about when Peabody was a young man, returning home after his early travels, with riches that surprised his father."

"Oh?" McGurk kept glancing at me as if to say, "Are you getting this down, Officer Rockaway?" And I kept glancing back as if to say, "I would be if I hadn't left my notebook and pen in the attic—as agreed !"

"Yes," Rob was saying. "And when his father pressed him to say how he had come by these riches, Jacob got angry and said, 'By cheating at cards, you old fool, so now you know!' "

"The respectable magistrate!" said Wanda.

"He was young, you must understand—"

"But *hitting* him?" McGurk urged. "His father?"

"Aye," said Rob. "The old man said he must give the fortune back to the men he had cheated. *That* was when Jacob struck him and ordered him to be silent."

"His own father!" murmured Mari.

"And that would mean the death penalty for him?" said McGurk. "Just hitting?"

"According to the Bible," said Rob. "But the old servant died last month, alas, and she was our only proof."

"What else does Hester have on him?" asked McGurk, blinking away his disappointment.

"Have on him?"

"Know about his—uh—evil deeds. As recorded in the book."

"Ah, one very serious thing!" Now Rob's eyes were gleaming. "I told her this."

"What?"

"That several years ago, Jacob Peabody sold—for many, many skins—muskets to some men in my tribe. While I was still with them. *And* rum."

"Oh, boy!" said McGurk. "Can you prove it?"

"Not yet," said Rob. " 'Twould be only my word against his. As one who was but a child. But one day I hope to find some adult member of my tribe who *will* speak about it."

We looked at one another. Hester Bidgood, Investigatrix, and her assistant seemed to have been very busy. McGurk looked deeply impressed. I bet if I'd had my typewriter with me he'd have been ordering me to make out ID cards for them. Officer Bidgood and Officer Scalp.

But then—look where their busy-ness had gotten *her*! . . .

McGurk moved on.

"This mysterious guest—"

"Micha Holroyd—yes," said Rob.

McGurk's eyes narrowed.

"Who?"

"Micha Holroyd. Peabody's guest."

"She found out his name then?"

"Yes. *I* did. Peabody brought him back to town earlier

this year. After he had been on a trip to England. But they were very secretive. The guest has never been beyond Peabody's gates. In summer he lived in the root cellar. Now, with colder nights, he lives in an attic."

"So how do you know his name?" said Brains.

"I have heard them talking," said Rob. "Most evenings, after dark, they stroll in the garden."

"But who—what is he here for?" said Willie.

"We know not," said Rob. "Yet there *is* a purpose. 'Your job,' Peabody has called it. 'When the time is ripe.' "

"Oh?"

"But only that," said Rob. "For that is when Holroyd always gets impatient and says, 'Yes, yes, yes! Leave that to me! In that field I am a master—*the* master—as you well know.' Those are his words."

McGurk seemed to have lost *his* words. He was staring out over the swamp like he was in a trance.

"And is that *all* he does?" said Wanda. "Come out for a stroll at night?"

"That and drink beer," said Rob. "Every day, in the middle of the afternoon, he sends to the tavern for a two gallon pitcher. Usually Peacemaker Cleary fetches it."

"What—what does this guy look like?" asked Willie.

"I only see him in the shadows," murmured Rob. "Very white—white skin—long white hair. Tall and thin, but greatly awry in his bearing. Like this."

Rob stood up and twisted his head to one side.

Then he straightened up, looked at the sky, and said: " 'Tis getting late. There *must* be some tidings now— good or bad. So please—go back now."

"What about you, Rob?" I said.

"I will come to you later, after dark, and cast a pebble against your window," he said. "Then *you* shall tell *me* what you have learned."

14 Rob's Report

We found Nell in tears in the kitchen.

Mr. Lawson and Mr. Phipps had just been for the second time that afternoon, after visiting Hester in jail.

"They seemed palsied, they did!" moaned Nell. "And is there any wonder?"

Hester was bearing up bravely, but very frightened. She had already been inspected for witchmarks by the Cleary women.

"Stripped naked and pored over, every inch, a terrible ordeal in itself . . ." sobbed Nell.

But they hadn't found anything—"no warts or moles, save for her freckles, poor lass"—and Hester had refused to confess or mention any names when Peabody himself had threatened and bullied her afterward.

"So . . . so she—" Nell concluded, nearly breaking down—"she is to be given the water test . . . at noon on Saturday. Which leaves her only tomorrow to—to—"

"Does Mistress Brown know?" McGurk asked.

"No, no!" cried Nell. "She be too weak! I gave her something to calm her and she is sleeping. Let her lay in peace, at least for now."

When we'd left Nell to recover and get on with preparing the meal, Wanda asked McGurk for more details.

"I know you mentioned the water test in your presentation, McGurk, but what exactly *do* they do?"

McGurk looked grave.

"Well, first they strip the—uh—accused person. Then they tie her right thumb to her left big toe. And her left thumb to the right toe. Okay? . . . And they do this tight, so she's bent double. Okay?"

Our murmurs were barely audible.

"Then, *two*, they wrap her in a blanket, all over, and tie it up with rope."

"So . . . she's all bundled up?" said Willie.

"Like a parcel, yes," said McGurk. "Which, *three*, they then put into deep water, a pond or a river. Then they watch to see if it sinks or floats. If it sinks, she's declared innocent—and much good that does her! Because then she's dead, of course. Drowned."

He was looking mad now.

"But if she *floats*," he went on, "why, then she's guilty of being a witch. And why? Because water *rejects* such evil persons. That's the cockamamie theory."

"Pre-preposterous!" gasped Brains.

"Yeah!" growled McGurk. "So then they feel it's okay

to go ahead and hang her. They feel that *that's* justice!"

He glared around at us.

"I'll tell you what else I read, too," he said. "The jerks often tried to make it so she *did* float. By laying it very gently on the water. Or tying a length of rope to the bundle so they could pull it along the surface. What they called 'swimming' it."

Dead silence.

Mari broke it.

"Correction, Chief McGurk. What they *call* swimming it."

"Huh?"

"*Call*, not *called*, Chief McGurk. It is happening now."

"Or soon will be," said Wanda.

McGurk's growl was the deepest yet.

"Not if *we* can help it!"

But he wasn't very sure *how* to help, when we asked him. None of us were. It was a gloomy meal we sat down to *that* evening. Even pumpkin pie didn't help.

Straight after it, we went up to the attic with a couple of lighted candles. It was quite dark outside by then. And we were just deciding how to break the terrible news to Rob when there was a soft owl hoot, followed by a tap on the window, which we quickly opened. He was already halfway up the ivy. As McGurk hauled him in, Rob's first words were: "Have you heard the news?"

"Yes. They—"

"They're going to give her the water test," said Rob. "I know. Saturday at noon."

"*How* do you know?" said McGurk.

"From the very source," said Rob, padding across to one of the chests and sitting down. "From the lips of Jacob Peabody himself. And Micha Holroyd. I have just come from them."

He looked strange. I don't mean just because of the mud he had smeared on his face—no doubt for camouflage—but the glow in his eyes. Not fierce. Fierce, I could have understood. No. This was a *triumphant* glow.

"I now think I know how I may be able to rescue her," he said. "At least there is a chance."

"Oh? What—how—"

" 'Twas Micha Holroyd himself who gave me hope. The wise man! The adviser!"

Then he told us what he'd overheard as the men had taken their evening stroll, and I must say he seemed to remember every word like it was all burned into his memory. I mean, it was as if we'd been there by his side, lurking in the shadows of that garden.

"See that she is wearing her shift when she is placed in the blanket," the crook-necked man had said.

"What difference will *that* make?" asked Peabody. "Naked or clad, the test will give us the truth."

The soft giggle then must have been horrible to hear. Rob shuddered as he mentioned it.

"Come! You know better than that, Jacob!" were Holroyd's next words.

Peabody began to bluster; Holroyd continued to snicker.

"Let me tell you *why* she must wear something, eh?"

"Why?"

"The better to conceal a small plank or hunk of bark."

"But that will help her float, man!"

" 'Twill indeed, Jacob. And so make *sure* she is proven a witch. That is what you desire, is it not?"

"Yes, but—you know very well that the sooner the wench is dead the safer are my secrets!"

"Patience, Jacob!" had been the answer. "She will still die, and soon. But on the gallows. As a proven witch."

"Yes, but—"

"But if she be drowned and proven innocent, the townspeople's consciences may prick them and cause their witch-hunting fever—so ably fanned by thy lecture—to cool mightily. What good will it be *then* to cry out against Mistress Brown and the others and demand *they* be hung for witching?"

Rob was silent for a while.

Then he looked up.

"That settled the matter for Peabody. And that is how they will proceed on Saturday."

"And you think it will make it easier to *rescue* her?" said McGurk.

"Yes," said Rob. "But I will still need your help."

"You've got it," said McGurk. "But—"

"Good. So listen and I will outline my plan. . . ."

As he did this, our spirits lifted. But only a little. I mean, it was so daring. And it depended so much on so many things.

"I have not worked out *all* the details yet," he said, as he prepared to leave. "But tomorrow I *will* have. Meet me at the alder tree by the swamp after you have eaten your nooning, and we will go over my plan then. Including your parts in it . . ."

Then he went over the sill and down the ivy and off into the darkness.

15 Blazing Scalp's Lodge

He was waiting for us when we got there the next afternoon.

"Is there any more news?" he asked.

We told him Nell had been to the jail that morning, and that Hester's aunt had refused to go with her, being scared out of her mind that she would be accused of witchcraft herself.

"That does not surprise me," he murmured. "She will probably blame *me* for Hester's plight."

She did already, according to Nell. But we didn't say so. Instead, we told him that Nell had taken Hester some extra food.

"But she didn't think Hester was eating anything," said Wanda.

"In fact, she's refusing to *speak* to anyone much," said Mari.

"And she isn't even *crying*," said Brains. "I guess the shock and the fear must have dried her up. It happens, sometimes."

Rob frowned.

"*That* will not help her cause. 'Tis taken for a witch sign, the inability to weep."

"Yes, well maybe that won't be important," said McGurk. "If we rescue her. Uh—you were going to tell us full details. . . ."

"Yes," said Rob. "But this is too important to discuss even here. We will go to my lodge."

"Lodge?" said McGurk.

"Over there," said Rob, pointing to the large clump of undergrowth and bushes, out in the middle of the swamp. "But be sure to follow me singly."

"In—uh—Indian file?" I said.

"Yes. The paths are narrow. One step either side and you are up to your waist in mud and water."

We must have looked uneasy. He grinned.

"But, for your further guidance, the way is marked."

"Oh?" said McGurk, looking across the swamp.

"Yes," said Rob. "Those branches. I said yesterday they had been blown there by the storm." He bowed slightly at Wanda. "Well, I lied. *I* put them there. They are the markers. If you go straight from one to the other in a certain order, 'twill take you safely to the lodge."

"Yeah, but *what* order?" said Wanda.

Rob smiled. It was a rather sad smile.

"By *ABC* order."

"Alphabetical?"

"Yes. 'Twas Hester's idea. She said 'twould help my schooling."

And, son of a gun, he was right! And no, none of the branches had been twisted into the shape of a letter. It was far cleverer than that. Here's the plan of that swamp that Wanda drew for our records:

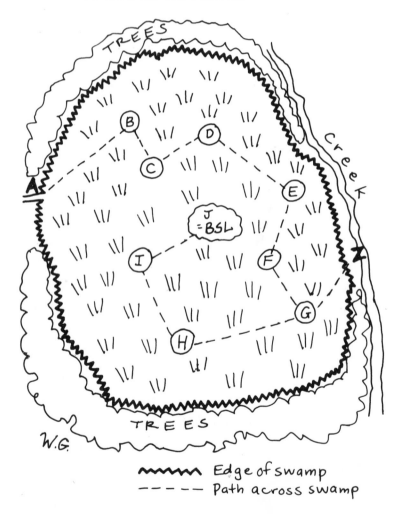

~~~~~ Edge of swamp
------ Path across swamp

A was of course the alder. The path, wet and looking like swamp itself, though firm enough, led first to the birch branch—still with its yellow leaves.

C was marked by the cedar branch that Wanda had queried yesterday and *D* by the spray of scarlet leaves on a dogwood branch. *E* was an elm branch, with yellow leaves and clusters of flat, brown keys. *F* was the fir, also queried by Wanda. *G*—where Brains missed his footing and got himself a shoeful of water—was groundsell. (Even I knew that one, with its fruit like clusters of little paintbrushes dipped in white.)

H I also knew, being holly. *I* nearly had Wanda fooled, seeing that it was holly again, until she remembered it was also called ilex. *J* was the lodge itself, with the bright orange-red leaves of the juneberry laid on top of some other branches.

And the Z I will tell you about later.

Most of us didn't know more than three or four of them, except Wanda. So I guess even if any stranger had come along and suspected a code, he wouldn't have gotten very far. Especially if he tried to get from *A* to *I* direct, or *C* to *J*, or something like that!

"Is this where you'll be bringing Hester?" asked Wanda, when we were all safely on the island (also marked B.S.L. for Blazing Scalp Lodge).

We were crouching under a canopy of branches and brushwood, which we could now see had been woven this way and that to make a pretty neat roof.

"Yes," said Rob. "If my plan is successful. Sit down," he said, pointing to the rushes strewn on the floor. "Around this."

"This" was a sort of square, shallow box, made out of roughly trimmed twigs at the sides and filled with a layer of drying mud. Three leaves were sticking out, making it look like he'd been trying to raise seedlings. But it wasn't anything to do with growing things. I soon realized this when I saw the familiar shape he'd drawn there with a finger or a stick.

This shape, the river shape:

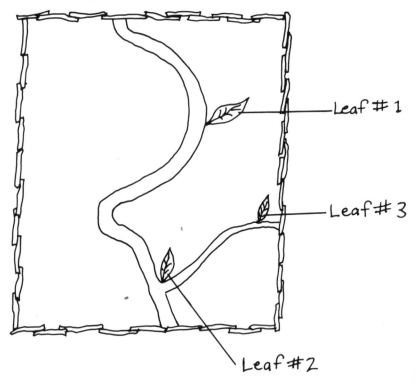

Leaf #1

Leaf #3

Leaf #2

Pointing with a twig, he began to outline his plans. "Here," he said, tapping Leaf #1, "is where they will be placing Hester in the river—where they usually launch their boats. . . . And here—" he tapped the groove at a point just opposite the leaf—"is where I will be waiting. Already in the water. Concealed by the overhanging bushes."

We listened in silence, trying to imagine the scene: the tied-up bundle, the onlookers, Peabody—probably holding the loose end of rope himself—the Clearys, and, unsuspected by them, the half-naked body of Hester's friend, lurking behind the leaves, a knife clamped between his teeth.

"Then, as soon as they have launched her, I will strike," he said. "I will sever the cord binding the blanket, then the cords between her hands and feet."

"But will you be able to do that fast enough?" said McGurk. "In the water and all?"

Rob's eyes flashed.

"As fast as this!" he hissed.

There were three more flashes as the knife swept down low among us. "Blanket-thumb-toe-thumb-toe!" he said, all in a single breath. And there—dangling limp, cut close to the knots—were the black sash-type belt that McGurk had on his doublet, Willie's left breeches' knee-ribbon, and my right shoe string.

"Even in water!" grunted Rob, replacing the knife in its sheath.

"Gee!" murmured McGurk, gaping at the severed knots. "That was neat! Go on, Blazing Scalp!"

He wasn't calling him by his European name now, note. And he wasn't being funny, either. He breathed that Indian name with the very greatest respect.

" 'Twill be done before they even know it," said Blazing Scalp. "And by then I will have borne Hester many, many yards away downstream. And when we have rounded this corner we shall be well out of sight, screened by the trees."

"What if they—?" Brains began.

"Even if they follow—which in truth, they will, and on horses, too, for there is a path along this bank—'twill be too late. Long before they reach the corner themselves, Hester and I will have diverted *here*. . . ."

He tapped the second leaf.

"*We* will be well along this creek, while *they* will continue on, over the plank bridge that spans the mouth of the creek and along the riverbank. They will expect us to go as far and as rapidly as possible, which means keeping to the river and its powerful currents."

"So this third leaf—" said McGurk.

"Is where I will bring Hester to the shore," said Blazing Scalp. He folded his arms and stared at us challengingly. "That is my plan."

After a few moments' silence, Wanda said: "And exactly whereabouts from here is the place you've marked with leaf number three?"

"Yonder," said Blazing Scalp, pointing. "At the edge of the swamp. Where that fallen log is. There is a path straight from it to the groundsell branch. Thence to the hollies and here."

The fallen log was where we've put a Z on the map, as well as on the swamp plan.

"I like it!" said McGurk, gleefully. "So what do you want *us* to do, Blazing?"

"Make sure there are towels and dry clothes for Hester," said our friend, beginning to sound gentler, more like Rob again.

"Towels, no problem," said McGurk. "But clothes? *Girls'* clothes?"

"That's no problem, either," said Wanda. "Nell should have some that'll fit. And if she doesn't," she added staunchly, "Hester can have my regular ones!"

McGurk gaped. The prospect of seeing Hester in Wanda's jeans and pink windbreaker was something else.

Rob didn't know anything about this, of course. "So some of you will be waiting by the log, ready for our arrival," he said.

"*Some* of us?" said McGurk.

"Yes," said Rob. "Because it is vital that at least one be *here*." He tapped the second leaf. "He or she or they will be concealed here. In some bushes I will show you to presently."

"Doing what?" said Brains.

"Keeping watch lest Hester and I be too closely pursued. To warn us of this."

"Warn you how?" asked McGurk.

"A shout and a wave will suffice," said Rob. "I will be alert for such a warning. But that is a very remote chance."

"Yeah, but what if it *does* happen that way?" said McGurk.

"Then we shall still proceed along the creek," said Rob, "but with even greater haste. . . . At least they will not be able to bring horses up here."

Brains was frowning.

"Okay," he said. "Let's suppose they don't see you come up here. Suppose they go galloping over the bridge and along the riverbank. Wouldn't it be useful to know that, too?"

"Well, yes. The lookout would then run and give us the good tidings—"

"From Leaf Two to Leaf Three? On what I bet is one lousy, soggy, rough path?" Brains glanced at his still very wet shoe.

"What are you getting at, Officer Bellingham?"

"Signals, McGurk," said Brains, pushing his glasses back along his nose.

"*Smoke* signals?" said Rob. "But that would require a tinder box and—and besides, the pursuers, too, would see such signals. Even if you could make them correctly," he added, looking doubtfully at Brains.

"Ah, yes!" said Brains. "They'd certainly see *smoke*, but—"

"But we have other ways," said McGurk, bursting to get in on the act. "I see what you mean, Officer Bellingham." He turned to Rob. "I don't want to get into it now, Blazing Scalp, but you'll see when the time comes. Trust me."

"Yeah!" said Brains. "And we could also be in touch with someone at Leaf One, to let the others know everything's running to schedule at that end."

Rob was looking from Brains to McGurk and back again. "This doth sound like magic. . . ."

"Not really, Blazing Scalp," said McGurk. "No more magic than guns must have seemed to you guys—uh—Indians, the first time." He grinned. "Just something else they sell all over Virginia nowadays. Anyway, you concentrate on your part. I mean, are you sure you can make it? Swimming all this way, with maybe a half-dead girl?"

" 'Tis naught!" Blazing Scalp drew himself up. "Was I not the best swimmer in my tribe when I was but twelve? I could swim twenty times the distance. Yea! And twenty times twenty, to save Hester!"

There was nothing to say to *that*. The only halfway replies were a murmured, soulful, "Ah!" from Mari and a deep, deep sigh from Wanda, whose eyes were shining unnaturally bright.

"Pull yourself together, Officer Grieg!" growled McGurk. "There's work to be done. Our client isn't home and dry *yet*!"

16 The Rescue

It was very quiet at the side of the creek the next morning. There was only the rippling of the water and a faint hissing. McGurk, Brains, and I were sitting on the fallen log, bending forward to listen to the two walkie-talkies on the ground. The hissing came from one of them—the one set to "Receive."

I thought about the rest of the Organization. Willie, perched behind the bushes on a bluff overlooking the mouth of the creek. He, too, had a couple of walkie-talkies, one set to "Receive" and the other to "Send." I hoped they were working okay. And Wanda and Mari, high in the willow tree we'd checked out the afternoon before—still leafy enough for concealment. They should be looking down now at the launching place, where the crowd would be gathering.

McGurk lifted up the set switched to "Send."

"Officers Grieg and Yoshimura. Are you—?"

"Receiving you pretty well, McGurk." Wanda's voice was faint and a bit sputtery, but clear enough. "The crowd is getting bigger. Can you hear the town crier's bell?"

We couldn't.

"Any sign of Hester yet?" said McGurk.

"No, but the minute there is, we'll let you know."

McGurk then contacted Willie.

"Do you receive me, Officer Sandowsky?"

There was some grunting—then: "Yeah—uh—loud and clear, McGurk."

"You okay there? You sound—"

"Just a wasp," said Willie. "It's moved on now."

"Well, wasp or no wasp, Officer Sandowsky, you stick to your post. It won't be long now. Are you hearing Officers Grieg and Yoshimura all right?"

Willie said he was.

Then: "McGurk, McGurk! Are *you* receiving *us*?"

It was Wanda again.

"Yes. What—?"

"They're bringing her out now—out from Main Street." Wanda sounded upset. "And they've already got her trussed in a blanket. Those horrible Cleary women are carrying it—grinning!"

"And now the crowd is parting," came Mari's voice, calmer but very grave. "Jacob Peabody is taking the end of the rope and the women are lowering the bundle into the water."

"Yeah! And so gently!" Wanda sounded disgusted. "Just like you said!"

That was when I began to wonder about Rob.

"Is Rob in place yet?" I said.

"He'd better be!" grunted McGurk.

"We can't *see* him," said Wanda.

"You're not supposed to," said McGurk. "Yet. But go on. Is the bundle in?"

"They've just let go of it," said Wanda. "And—oh—this horrible crowd! Can you hear them? Sort of cheering, but quietly. A nasty, gloating sound like—"

"It is beginning to sink," Mari cut in. "Oh, dear! It—it—"

"But no!" said Wanda. "There it is! It's floating! Peabody's still holding the rope. It's beginning to tighten. The bundle's floating out from the shore. We can't see Rob yet. Oh, I do hope he hasn't been held up—"

"No! No!" came Mari's voice, excited now. "Look! The V in the water. Like a beaver. Straight for Hester!"

Now we could hear background cries. Yells of surprise and anger.

"I see his arm," said Wanda. "A knife. It's him! He's slashed the rope around the bundle. And—ha!—Peabody's fallen on his back, holding the empty rope!"

"And the blanket has fallen away," said Mari. "Something white has—it is Hester! She is free . . . but . . . but she is floundering."

"Yes, but he's steadied her, he's steadied her! He's got her head above water and—wow!—he's sweeping her along in midstream! What—what is it, Mari?"

"The man Cleary has just pointed his gun at them, but Peabody has knocked it down. He is waving his arms and shouting. For horses, I think."

"Yeah, but now Hester and Rob are almost at the bend. And—yes—there they go. Oh, I do hope they make it! Over to you, Willie. . . ."

"Yes," came Willie's clearer voice. "Yes. I see them. It's them. White cloth. His head. Hers. Getting closer."

"Anyone on the path yet?" said McGurk. "Following them?"

"No. . . . Not a soul. And now they're just under me. Moving into the creek. They—they're swirling around and around. She seems in trouble. I hope he knows what he's doing."

"So do I!" muttered McGurk.

"But—hey!" said Willie. "It's okay. It's okay, McGurk! They've made it! He's half out of the water. He's standing up. Dragging her. She looks all in. And now he's lifting her. He's carrying her along the creek. And now I can't see them for the bushes."

"Anyone in pursuit *yet*?" said McGurk.

"No—not—hold it!" Willie sounded alarmed. "Someone on a horse. And another. And *another*. . . . But they won't be able to see Rob and Hester. Not from there. *Will* they? But no. There they go now . . . first guy . . . second . . . the others. Over the bridge. Downriver."

"Good work, Officer Sandowsky! Keep looking, though, and—"

McGurk broke off.

There'd been a shrill jay screech and Rob was just staggering into view, supporting Hester.

We ran to meet them.

She was very pale, dripping wet, the nightgown sticking to her. She was coughing and spluttering and wheezing. Rob looked in better shape, though breathing heavily. He was naked except for a short leather apron (the sort you see Indians wearing in pictures) with a belt and the knife in its sheath. He seemed to have smothered himself all over with a thick, reddish-yellow grease. It made him look more of an Indian than ever, especially with his hair now darkened by water.

But it was Rob, rather than Blazing Scalp, who looked at us with such anxiety. "Your signals . . . whatever they are . . . do they . . . have they . . .?"

"It's okay," said McGurk. "No one's following. Not yet, anyway. The clothes and towels are behind the log."

"Good!" said Rob, leading Hester to them. "Are you

able to do it yourself, Hester? I had thought the two girls would be here, but—"

"Yes, yes," she gasped, her teeth beginning to chatter. "Now please . . . turn the other way. . . ."

"For sure!" said Rob. "You three, also—"

But he needn't have worried. We were already facing the way they'd come, alert for the least sound or sight of pursuit.

"I wish she'd hurry up!" muttered McGurk. "The sooner they're over in that lodge, out of sight, the better I'll like it!"

Hester must have felt the same. In less than a couple of minutes, she called out that she was ready. Still looking rather damp and pale, but dressed in the clothes that Nell had sorted out for her, she came to Rob's side.

"I am ready now," she said, giving us a friendly, but still rather scared look. "Do these know of the lodge?"

"Yes. Can you walk there?"

"I—I think so. If you support me, Rob." She was still looking at us curiously. "Do they know about Jacob Peabody and—?"

"They know everything. They are our friends. They have helped in your escape."

Hester nodded. Her eyes lightened some. She was just getting ready to say something when suddenly, one of the walkie-talkies sputtered and Wanda's voice came through, weakly but urgently.

"*May Day! May Day! We—*"

Brains had bent and killed it, but not soon enough.

The scared look had leaped back into Hester's eyes, wide with wonder now. Rob wasn't looking any too serene, either. But McGurk was quick to take charge.

"Don't waste time. Get over there. We're going back to town to make sure Jacob Peabody never troubles Hester again. Or his buddy, Micha Holroyd!"

McGurk sounded so sure that, with one last, curious glance at the now silent black box, Rob nodded. Hester, however, burst into tears.

"Oh, I am so glad!" she wailed.

"This is where we came in, men," murmured McGurk, as we watched Rob steer the weeping Hester across the swamp paths, walking close behind her, holding her shoulders.

"She's relieved," said Brains. "I told you. She *can* cry now."

When we were sure the fugitives had made it and were out of sight, I turned to McGurk.

"How can you be so sure?" I said. "About Peabody and Holroyd?"

"You'll see," he said. "But come on. We'll go pick up Officer Sandowsky. And switch that set on again. Officer Grieg sounded like they're in some kind of trouble. *Big* trouble! Officers-in-need-of-assistance trouble!"

17 Peacemaker Makes a Deal

We tried to get Wanda and Mari on the walkie-talkies several times on our way back, but no luck.

So we were much relieved on reaching Mistress Brown's to find them safe, up in the attic.

But Wanda was very pale.

"Everything okay?" she asked, in a low, scared voice.

"Yes," said McGurk. "But what about you two?"

Wanda sighed.

"You tell him, Mari."

"It was Peacemaker Cleary, Chief McGurk. He was there at the foot of the tree when we climbed down."

"His eyes were popping out of his head," said Wanda. "Tell them what he said, Mari."

The imitation that followed was uncanny. Just like Peacemaker Cleary was in the room.

" *I see 'ee! I see 'ee! Talking to Satan's imps in them black witches' wallets!* "

"Oh, no!" groaned Brains.

"Then he came to snatch mine off me," said Wanda. "And I—I lost my head and started calling 'May Day.' As if *that* could have helped. But luckily, Mari got behind him and put him in an arm lock."

"Good work, Officer Yoshimura," murmured McGurk, acknowledging another of Mari's skills. "But go on. What about witnesses? Was it just Peacemaker—?"

"Yes, thank goodness!" said Wanda. "Everyone else was too busy milling around trying to get a sight of Rob and Hester. Or running off to get horses."

"So what happened with Peacemaker Cleary?" I asked.

"Well, he backed off, but—"

"He had torn Wanda's collar," said Mari. "And pulled her dress off her shoulder."

"Yeah!" grunted Wanda. "Just enough to expose my beauty spot. The clover leaf."

"Then he cried out again," said Mari. " *'I see it! I see it! There! Her witch's mark!'* "

"Great!" groaned McGurk.

"Luckily, no one was taking any notice," said Wanda. "And just then his father grabbed him and said Mr. Peabody wanted him to see Mr. Holroyd safely home."

"*Mr. Holroyd?*" gasped McGurk.

"Yes," said Wanda. "Muffled up. All in black—cloak, hat, scarf. He was very slow and twisted looking. He'd been there all the time, next to Peabody. We didn't realize who it was—"

"Yeah! The adviser!" McGurk looked excited. "The expert! He'd come out of his lair for *that*, you can bet on it!"

"Anyway," said Wanda, "Peacemaker had to lead him away. But not before he turned and said—go on, Mari."

" *'You wait!'* " said Mari in her Peacemaker voice. " *'You wait until Mr. Peabody gets back with them other two witches! Wait until I tell him!'* "

"Oh, boy!" said Willie. "So next it'll be you two we'll have to rescue!"

"Take it easy!" said McGurk. "There'll be no need. Jacob Peabody will be exposed himself before today's out."

"Yes, McGurk!" I said. "Tell us why you're so sure."

Just then, Nell called up to say the meal was ready.

"Later," murmured McGurk.

The meal was beef potpie with biscuits on top instead of a crust. Delicious.

Nell served us herself, after making sure the other servants were out of the way.

"Is—is all well?" she asked.

We'd had to tell her about the rescue attempt when we'd asked her for spare clothes and towels. But no details. No places or times. "Strictly on a need-to-know basis, men," McGurk had warned. But he needn't have worried. "I do not want to know exact particulars," Nell had said. "Lest something go wrong and they take me and torture me. Then I *could* not tell them anything, even if I would."

One very brave lady, in her own quiet way.

McGurk said, "Yes, ma'am. All *is* well."

"They—they are safe?"

"Yes."

"And well hid?"

"*Very* well hid."

"Thank the good Lord for that! . . . Oh, and you, of course! Thank 'ee all. . . . And now I must go into town. I hear they have put Rob's grandparents in jail. I must see if this be true."

"Yes," said McGurk. "And keep your ears open, Nell. Then let us know what's going on. Any news of the chase."

When Nell had gone and we were finishing our meal, we asked McGurk about his plans.

"Not yet," he said. "Not until Nell gets back and we have the latest situation report."

"But—"

"Not *now*, Officer Grieg!" he insisted, waving a corn stick.

And he meant it. Nothing would shake him. All we had to console ourselves with was a certain gleam in his eyes—that cat-about-to-pounce gleam—as he munched away. A sure sign he was onto something big.

Only after Nell had come back, nearly an hour later, did he spring into action.

The news? Just that:

1. Mr. and Mrs. MacGregor had not been jailed—yet.

2. More men with horses had been sent for.

3. Others were setting out on foot, with guns and sticks.

4. Not everyone was going. Many were staying home, keeping out of it.

5. Others, still, were drinking in Cleary's tavern, gossiping and gloating and guessing what might happen.

"Fat Goody Cleary and that horrid Peacemaker are being kept very busy," Nell concluded. "The Devil is surely finding work for idle hands—and idle tongues—*this* day!"

But McGurk seemed very satisfied. "Right, men," he said. "This is where we make our move!"

Exactly where we made our move wasn't far away. Just four or five hundred yards across the fields. Here's a blowup of that area based on Wanda's map. I have marked the spot with an asterisk:

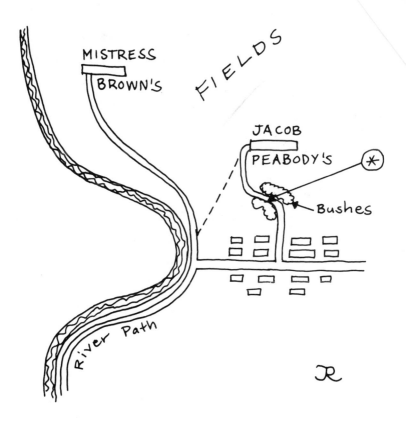

It was on the track leading from Jacob Peabody's place, at a point where there was a small stand of trees and some bushes at the side.

We kept behind these, watching the track.

It was very quiet.

We could hear singing, rowdy but faint—coming from the tavern, we guessed.

McGurk still refused to answer most of our questions,

except to say he was looking out for Peacemaker Cleary, on his regular errand with Micha Holroyd's beer.

"Peacemaker Cleary?" said Wanda. "What—what do you want *him* for?"

"You'll see," murmured McGurk, fumbling with something in his pocket.

"Maybe he'll be too busy today," said Brains. "You heard Nell."

"He won't be too busy for *this* errand," said McGurk.

Maybe there *wasn't* anything in his pocket, I thought. Maybe he was just crossing his fingers.

Then—after about half an hour, when McGurk was beginning to look worried—Peacemaker Cleary came into sight.

He was walking slowly, eyes on a large pewter jug he was carrying. It looked heavy, the way his elbows were bent. Also very full, judging from the way he stopped and took a long, slurping sip.

"Hey!" said McGurk, stepping out into the track. "He won't like *that*!'

"What be that to you?" said Peacemaker, looking startled. " 'Twould only have spilled over and gone to waste."

"Hm!" said McGurk. "We can't let *that* happen, can we?"

He made no attempt to stand aside. Instead, he brought something from his pocket and held it up.

The Swiss Army knife!

"Hey!" gasped Brains. "My knife!"

We were *all* surprised, especially at McGurk's next words: "How would you like to own this fine Virginia knife, Peacemaker?"

Peacemaker's eyes had been bulging with fear. Now they bulged even further, but this time with greed. A slow smile began to spread over his face. He put the jug on the ground.

"Me?" he said, reaching out. "That?"

McGurk drew it back.

"There are conditions," he said.

Well! Every man has his price, they say. And now I reckon it goes for kids, too. I mean, you should have seen and heard McGurk bargaining with *that* kid!

Peacemaker had already been softened up by the horses' hooves thing, remember. And as McGurk fanned out the various gizmos, slowly, one at a time, Peacemaker's face was a picture.

The two blades, the gimlet, the glass cutter, and the bottle opener made his eyes glisten, even though he couldn't possibly have known what some of them were for. With the file—smooth side, rough side—he was drooling. And by the time McGurk had flourished the corkscrew, he was sold.

"Gimme that," he said, reaching out again, "and I will

do anything you want. You want me to keep quiet about her witchmark?"

"That," said McGurk, "and one other little thing."

"Content!" said Peacemaker, still with his grubby hand out. "Come! Tell me! What?"

"Just this. Check Mr. Holroyd out. See if *he* has a witchmark. On his left foot."

Peacemaker's jaw dropped.

"But—why? How?"

"Never mind why," said McGurk. "Here's how. . . ."

He bent forward and whispered in Peacemaker's ear.

Peacemaker's eyes popped, and a lopsided grin crept over his face again.

"Ha! Yea! But—"

"If you *don't* want this fine, red knife, of course—" said McGurk, stepping back.

"No! No! I mean yes! Content! Content! I will do it! I will do it!"

He picked up the jug, slopping the beer, and hurried on his way, turning every few steps to say, "You promise?"

"I promise," said McGurk, gently waving the knife.

"Hey, McGurk!" said Brains. "You don't really mean to give it to him, do you?"

"You bet I do, Officer Bellingham! If he comes back with the information I'm hoping for."

"But—"

"It will help to save lives. Including Officer Grieg's, maybe."

About twenty minutes later, Peacemaker came running back, swinging the empty jug.

"Say! It worked! It worked!"

"You—uh—*accidentally* spilled the beer all down the inside of his left boot?"

"I surely did!"

"And?"

"And he cussed me and aimed a blow, but I ducked."

"And?"

"He pulled his boot off, like you said."

"And?"

"Then he pulled his stocking off."

"And?"

"And then I see it! His foot was like to be black, 'twas so dirty—"

"Call that a *witchmark*?!" said Brains, glancing wildly at his knife, still in McGurk's hand.

"No," said Peacemaker. "But his two smallest toes was! They was stuck together, like a duck's!"

"Terrific!" breathed McGurk, eyes glowing.

"You want me to cry out on him for being a witch?" said Peacemaker. "For the knife and *his* spectacles, I would!"

The jerk was looking at me.

"That won't be necessary," said McGurk. "Here's the knife. You've earned it."

Peacemaker snatched it and kissed it, and he was just turning to go when another of the town kids came running up. The sweat was in rivulets down his dusty forehead and cheeks.

"Peacie, Peacie!" he gasped. "They are found! They are hiding in South Creek swamp! Mr. Peabody—he hath sent some to call out the townsfolk and me to call out all his hands. . . . All the able-bodied ones . . . the women, too! To—to tell them to make haste . . . to bring guns . . . tinder boxes. . . . to help to smoke they witches out, if needs be!"

"Wait for me!" cried Peacemaker, an unholy glee in his eyes now.

And, flinging the jug to the side of the track, he ran after the other kid toward the house.

He'd kept a tight clutch on the knife, though.

"There!" growled Brains. "What if he goes and stabs Hester with it, McGurk? Huh? Our *client*! *My* knife!"

18 The Witchfinder Found

We were all aghast except McGurk.

He was gazing at the Peabody house, watching the two kids hammer on the door.

"Hester and Rob haven't been recaptured *yet*," he said.

"Yes, but—"

"It'll take hours to get them out of that swamp," he said. "You've seen the place."

"So what next?" I said.

"We set about getting Micha Holroyd out of *his* den. Once he's all on his own."

People were now hurrying from the house, heading straight across the fields for the river path. The sun was setting and the sky was blood red. Soon it would be dark.

While we watched, I asked McGurk how he'd guessed that Micha Holroyd had had such a birthmark.

"Micha Holroyd?" he said. "What Micha Holroyd?"

We stared. Was he losing his marbles?

He smiled back grimly.

"Remember what I was saying about fugitives? Sticking to their old initials even when they change their names? *And* the same number of syllables, I could have added."

"Syllables?" I said.

"Yeah. John Dix-well, James Dav-ids. . . . Mi-cha Hol-royd, Mat-thew Hop-kins."

"You mean the English guy?" said Wanda. "The—the Witchfinder General?"

"You bet!" said McGurk.

"But what makes you suspect *him*?" said Brains.

"And what makes you so sure?" said Wanda. "Sure enough to—"

"The age, for starters," said McGurk. "Hopkins would be just that age now. Plus, Micha Holroyd *is* an Englishman. *And* he seems to know all about testing witches."

"I'll be darned!" whispered Willie.

"I don't know for certain," McGurk went on. "But I bet Peabody brought him over for his expert advice and input. Like the gang bosses in New York used to bring in hit men from Detroit."

"But I thought you said he was *dead*, McGurk," Wanda protested. "In your presentation. That he'd been tried as a witch himself."

"Yes," said McGurk, frowning now. "When some English minister exposed him and said *he* must be in cahoots with the Devil to know so much about witches. And sure enough, they found the witchmark on his foot. Just an ordinary deformity, really."

"Yes," said Wanda. "But *you* said he was given his own water test and he floated and was condemned."

"True," said McGurk. "But the book I read said it wasn't clear what happened after that. Some say he was collared by a mob and lynched. Others say he got away. Cut down from the gallows by some of his goons, then went into hiding." He nodded grimly across to the Peabody house. "Well, now we know that *was* what must have happened."

I shuddered, thinking of the crooked neck.

"But how can we prove it?" said Brains.

"I'm not sure." McGurk was still frowning. "I *would* be sure, though. If only I could get hold of that book."

Wanda gave her head a scornful toss.

"Well, why worry, McGurk? The library'll be open in about thirty minutes. Thirty minutes and three hundred years!"

"Don't get smart, Officer Grieg!"

"Who're *you* calling smart?" she snapped back. "You have the gall to stand there talking about some library book while . . . why? What's wrong, McGurk?"

She was staring at the sudden broad, crazy grin lighting up his face.

"Nothing, Officer Grieg! I could—I could *kiss* you, Officer Grieg!"

"Hey, now!" said Wanda, stepping back. "Don't get carried away! I mean—"

"You've just given me the answer! Saying that about gall! That was the guy's name! The guy who denounced Hopkins back in England. The Reverend Mr. Gaule!"

He swung to Mari.

"Officer Yoshimura. You've heard the way these people talk. Do you think you could imitate the voice of an English minister from the middle of this century?"

"I—I will give it a good try," said Mari.

"Maybe even two English ministers, one a lot older than the other? *Very* old. Like—like he'd just returned from the grave?"

Mari wasn't fazed, even by *that*.

"If I can do one, Chief McGurk, I will be able to do the other."

"Great!" said McGurk. "So here's what we do now. . . ."

Ten minutes later, we were standing outside the main door of the Peabody house. McGurk had already explained about the other minister, a poor old man called Lowes, whom Hopkins had had condemned and executed, and who'd been made to repeat his own funeral service on the way to the scaffold.

The door had been left ajar by the servants in their hurry. The stairs were directly ahead of us. It was getting dark in there.

"Anybody home?" McGurk called out.

There was a stirring up above. The sound of a latch. The creak of a door. Then: "Where *is* everybody?" a thin, peevish voice came down. "Where is that fool with my beer?"

"I know not, Mr. Holroyd, sir." McGurk wasn't doing so badly with a seventeenth-century voice himself. "But there be two gentlemen wanting to see you, sir."

The door above creaked again.

"Eh? What gentlemen?"

Suddenly cautious.

"Traveled a long way, they have, sir," said McGurk. "All the way from England."

Silence. Another creak.

"Two *ministers*, sir," McGurk persisted. "The Reverend John Gaule from Huntingdon. And—uh—the Reverend John Lowes, sir, from Suffolk—and a very queer person he be." McGurk had to raise his voice here because, after what sounded like a gasp, the creaking door was slammed shut and the latch clicked and there was a padding of feet. "All bundled up, he be, sir, like in a dark, twisty sheet!"

"No, no!" came the faint, frightened voice. "I know them not! Send them away!"

●

McGurk nodded to Mari. She went up a couple of stairs.

"Come along, Hopkins!" she said, in a stern, male English voice. "The game is up, man!"

At the name "Hopkins" there'd been a yelp and more shuffling. It sounded like the unmasked witchfinder was backing way from the attic door as far as he could get.

Mari took another two steps and said, in the weirdest voice I have ever heard, frail and quavery but very penetrating: *"Yes, indeed, Hopkins! Dost not remember meee? . . . Lowes. . . . The poor, innocent wretch thou had put to death. . . . In sixteen hundred and forty-five? . . . Now I wish to . . . to speak with thee!"*

The menace in those last four words was something else again.

It certainly brought results.

First, a hoarse scream and a crash of broken glass.

Then another short silence, followed by louder screams. And then the sound of the attic door bursting open, followed by a rush of air from the main door behind us, and billowing flames suddenly lighting up the top of the stairs.

He must have knocked over an oil lamp.

And then he came slithering and stumbling down, screaming, half undressed, barefooted. He'd probably been waiting for his left boot and stocking to dry.

"No! No! Peabody! Save me!"

We backed toward the door.

"Look at that foot, men!" said McGurk. "It *is*—it really *is*—Matthew Hopkins!"

"Save me! Save me!" babbled the man. The flames were roaring. I remembered Nell's warning about how these houses had thickly thatched roofs. Hopkins was now on his knees, his white hair flying in the draft, clutching McGurk's legs. "Do not let them get me!"

"Come on," said McGurk. "Let's get him outa here before we *all* fry!"

Some of the townsfolk were already gathering outside. These were the people who hadn't gone to "smoke out" the fugitives. These were the decent ones who'd seen the flames and come to *help* a neighbor in trouble, not gloat. Some were already filling buckets at the well, but it was too late. Step by step, everyone was backing away from the inferno, including us and the still babbling Hopkins. Then: "What is this?" said a grave voice.

We turned and saw Mr. Lawson, accompanied by Mr. Phipps. They were staring at the man, who was back on his knees.

"Oh, sir!" yelped Hopkins, addressing the minister. "Thank heaven! *You* can save me, surely! I . . . I . . ."

And then, in a rush, out came his confession—who he really was, why Peabody had brought him here, how he was poor and frail and weak and had given in to Peabody's plans.

Mr. Lawson looked very grim in that flickering and pulsing firelight. I think he'd been waiting for a chance like this. A slow man, maybe, and not very courageous, but very, very firm and formidable when he did act.

"So!" he began, when Hopkins had blubbered to a stop. "*This* is what Master Peabody has been—"

He stopped as someone came running up, saying, "They are here! They are back!" It was Peacemaker, so full of news he seemed hardly to have noticed the flames behind us. "They smoked that Injun out with a Injun trick! Oh, Lordy, 'twas good! They made bows and shot flaming arrows to the roof of that den of theirs! 'Twent up in a great blaze, it did, and the witches they come out over their secret paths, and—"

Suddenly, Peacemaker stopped and stared.

"But *this* be ablaze, too! I thought 'twas a bonfire Mr. Peabody had ordered! Ready to roast the witches! But 'tis his *house!*"

"Yes, it *is* his house," said Mr. Lawson. "What is left of it."

He had turned toward the track, where a grim procession had come to a halt. Peabody was just dismounting from his horse. The older Clearys were still on theirs. Between them stood Rob and Hester, in chains, gaping at us. So were the rest of the crowd that had marched, no doubt in gleeful triumph, from South Creek swamp.

"My house!" gasped Peabody, darting forward.

" 'Tis too late, man!" said Mr. Lawson, putting out an arm.

Peabody looked at him. "But—" Then he saw the cringing Hopkins. "*Thou!*" he said, "So this is *thy* doing, drunken wretch!"

"Be still with thy bluster, Peabody!" thundered Mr. Lawson. "We know all now. From the lips of this, thy creature. I have a mind to arrest and punish thee myself. Now. This instant. For conspiracy. Conspiracy with this one to have Mistress Brown wrongfully hanged as a witch and her property confiscated, for you to buy cheap. Murther, no less! And for inciting and inflaming the populace . . . and . . ."

And so he went on, throwing the book at Peabody in front of that now silent crowd, with Peabody silent too, and scared—getting to look more and more like his cringing associate.

A chain clinked.

"*And free those two innocents!*" Mr. Lawson roared. "*Now! Instantly!*"

The Cleary brothers stumbled over themselves in their haste to obey.

Then Mr. Lawson resumed.

"Yes, wretch, yourself!" he growled at Peabody. " 'Tis *thou* who hast been a stranger in our midst. But we will not be like thee. We will let thee go and leave it to God to deal out thy just punishment!"

"That's what all crooks just *love* to hear!" muttered McGurk, looking less satisfied all at once.

"Oh, thank you, thank you, Luke!" Peabody was saying.

"There you are!" grumbled McGurk.

But Mr. Lawson wasn't through yet.

"On one condition!" he said. "You give up your land to be confiscated by the township. And you take thyself and that—*that* one—with thee, back to England. This very night. And you will be escorted to Boston by two of our best marshalls—no, not you, Ezra and Zeke Cleary, who art herewith relieved of your duties! Two of our *best* marshalls, Peabody, who will make sure that thou art detained there until a boat be available."

"That's more like it!" McGurk muttered. "*Much* more—"

Someone had tugged his sleeve.

Nell.

"Mistress Brown has heard," she said. "Come. She wishes to see you all, without delay."

1⑨ New Light on Hester

Before we went into Mistress Brown's bedroom, Nell asked us to change back into our own clothes and bring the "black boxes."

"She says she wishes to see you as you were when she saw you first, as a young girl," said Nell, shaking her head. "I fear she is losing her wits with the joy of these tidings."

But Gwyneth looked sane enough, sitting up in bed. And it was a big relief to be back in our familiar clothes.

"Ah, that is how I have always remembered you!" she said.

She looked more like the Gwyneth we had known, with that wide broad-lipped smile.

"You have done well," she said. "Sir Jack . . . Sir Joey . . . Lady Wanda . . . Lady Mari . . . Sir Willie . . . Master Brains . . ."

She gave each of us a long, glowing look as she spoke our names, her voice getting fainter and fainter.

Then she sighed and closed her eyes.

"Thy mission has been well and truly accomplished," she murmured.

Her words seemed to echo, but in a different voice. Stronger, brisker, male. Less full of relief. It was more like the voice of a school-bus driver who'd been running late and was hustling us on board. The Voice of the Black Boxes.

And even as we looked down at the walkie-talkies, everything began to spin, and it was like fallen leaves in a sudden blast of wind. All the reds, golds, yellows, oranges, and rusty browns of a New England fall, whirling faster and faster, blotting out every other sight.

But not sound—because I kept hearing cries of "I see 'ee!" and "They must be destroyed!" and "There are strangers in our midst!" and "I have a list!" Then came the deeper, steadier sound of sobbing, and this, too, faded and all became black. . . .

When I opened my eyes I was back in my own bed, the covers scattered on the floor.

It was the same with the whole Organization. Just like last time. All back in our own beds, as usual, after six or seven hours.

Three days had gone by, back in that early township.

Brains is still trying to work it out. A day for every hundred years traveled? Or a century for every two hours of sleep? Or what?

And that was like last time, also. The way it left us in two minds. I mean, if it *had* been a dream, it was shared by all six of us down to every last detail. We compared notes very carefully.

Most of us believed the walkie-talkies really were time machines.

Willie claimed this time he could detect a faint—ultra-faint—smell from the earlier century. An odor of apples and lavender lingering on the clothes that had been stashed in those chests. None of us others could, but we don't have Willie's nose.

Then there were the bug bites. We all had them, but they *could* have been made by modern bugs during the last few weeks of Indian summer. As McGurk said: "I guess the jury's still out on that one, men."

I thought *I* had proof positive, though. Those uneven, every-which-way lines of the only notes I managed to make, back on the mission. Caused by bad light and itchy clothes.

But Wanda said it was just the sort of writing someone could have done in the dark while sleepwalking. I said not. McGurk made me put it to the test by keeping my eyes shut while I wrote some more notes. These:

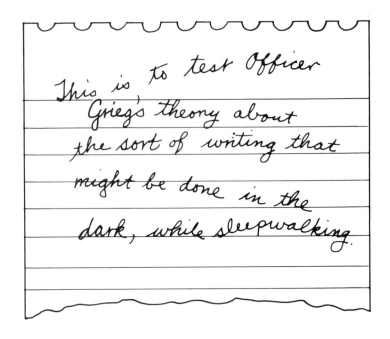

This is, to test Officer Grieg's theory about the sort of writing that might be done in the dark, while sleepwalking.

"There you are!" said Wanda.

"But I *don't* walk in my sleep!" I protested.

"How d'you know, if you're asleep?" said Wanda.

Anyway, dream or time trip, it was a *very* remarkable thing, and we all agreed there must have been *something* about Brains's walkie-talkies. He, of course, was all for the time trip theory. As proof, he swore he couldn't find his Swiss Army knife. But Wanda—Wanda again!—pointed out that he was biased.

"I mean, I'm not saying he's lying. But he *could* have misplaced it. I haven't seen him with it for days. In *this* century, I mean."

"Well, I don't care," said Brains. "I *know* Peacemaker Cleary has it. And I'll expect the Organization to buy me a new one out of the slush fund!"

"Sure thing, Officer Bellingham," said McGurk, a firm believer in the time trip theory.

As for Mari, she said she'd never heard many of those old English words before.

"So I could not possibly have dreamed them up, Chief McGurk!"

Even Wanda couldn't find an argument against *that*.

But maybe the best proof came a few days later in school.

"I've been doing some research of my own, class," said Ms. Ellis, as we were all working in our groups. "I have found out more about the girl Hester Bidgood."

Naturally, we were all ears.

"It seems she must have been acquitted of being a witch, after all. . . ."

"Tell us about it!" whispered McGurk, winking at us.

"I've come across part of the town register for 1696," said Ms. Ellis. "And she's down as Hester Bidgood, age seventeen, marrying a Robert MacGregor, age nineteen."

"Wow!" gasped Wanda.

"Are you *sure* that's MacGregor, Ms. Ellis?" said McGurk. "Not McGurk?"

"McGurk!" whispered Wanda. "You never give up,

do you? And even if McGurk had turned out to be Rob's real name, you know what it would have meant?"

"What, Officer Grieg?"

"That you could have gotten your red hair and freckles from either of them. But the *detective* skills would have been definitely from Hester. A woman!"

"Huh!" was all he could say to that.

A few days later, Ms. Ellis came up with another new fact.

"Hester again, class! I've found some more information. . . . This was from the 1699 records, the year Hester became twenty-one. Apparently, she had been awarded a large sum of money and a considerable tract of land, to be handed over to her at that age. Maybe as compensation for false arrest. It doesn't say. . . ."

This caused a stir among the Organization.

"And, class," Ms. Ellis went on, "do you know what that young Mrs. MacGregor did? She made it all over to found a hospital. The Hester MacGregor Hospital for Aged and Infirm Widows and Spinsters. Old ladies who, not much earlier, might have been cruelly persecuted and put to death as witches."

"Is that the same as the MacGregor Residential Homes for Seniors, miss?" someone asked. "Over the other side of Willow Park, near where the old town was?"

"Yes," said Ms. Ellis. "That's what it's called now. And

of course, today it's a group of very beautiful modern bungalows, not a hospital."

"Ms. Ellis!"

It was Sandra Ennis. Her lopsided grin just then had a strong look of Peacemaker Cleary's.

"Yes, Sandra?"

"Wanda Grieg's crying!"

Wanda had been blowing hard into a limp tissue.

"*Who's* crying?" she said.

"You are!" said Sandra. "There are tears in your eyes *now*!"

"You want a punch on the nose?" growled Wanda. "Then there'll be tears in *your* eyes!"

"Wanda!" said Ms. Ellis.

"Yeah, Officer Grieg!" said McGurk. "Cut it out. . . . I guess she has a soft spot for Hester, Ms. Ellis. Being a sister detective and all."

But that wasn't the only reason McGurk had apologized for his officer. *He'd* been getting a soft spot, too. For Ms. Ellis, no less. On account of all her excellent detective work.

In fact, as he told us after school, he'd actually been thinking of making her an honorary member of the McGurk Organization. And getting me to make out an ID card for her.

I mean: "Officer Ms. Ellis," yet!

But that was going over the top, even for McGurk.

So when he'd simmered down, he had me type out the new card for the Organization notice instead:

RECYCLED

RACKETEERS   REVEALED

To which (never satisfied, as usual!) he added, in his own hand:

And Pursued
with
Perseverance